Sentenced to Heaven

Ellis Elms

U Fiction Publishing LLC

Published by U Fiction Publishing LLC.

Paperback ISBN: 979-8-9941212-0-7

First Edition

Author website: www.elliselms.com

Contents

13

YES, THIRTEEN

PART ONE

THE WAITING ROOM

U Fiction Publishing LLC

Episode 1

The Judge

The first thing Judge Arthur Blackwell noticed was the hum.

It wasn't the celestial hum of a choir. It was the 60-cycle, ballast-in-a-dying-fluorescent-light hum of a public utility. He had died, he was sure of that—a massive, gavel-slamming coronary right in the middle of sentencing a fraudster to eight years for securities fraud. He had expected light. Or darkness. Or, at the very least, some dignity.

He did not expect a beige waiting room with plastic, butt-molded chairs.

A Muzak version of "Stairway to Heaven" was being muttered by a tiny speaker in the corner. The fluorescent lights buzzed with that particular frequency that suggested they'd been installed sometime during the Carter administration and had been dying ever since.

And there was a machine. Like at the deli. Red plastic. Slightly cracked.

TAKE A NUMBER

Arthur took one. 847,293.

He sat, smoothing the lapels of a suit he hadn't died in—strange, that—and waited. He was a man of order, of rules, of procedure. This place, whatever it was, clearly had a system. There would be processing. There would be recognition. There would be vindication.

He scanned the room, his mind instinctively cataloging the others. Judging.

There was a man, tattooed and hard-eyed, sitting with a terrifying stillness. Mid-forties, maybe. Prison ink on his knuckles. A lifer, Arthur diagnosed immediately. Violent offender. Probably here for the same-day express to the downstairs department.

There was an old woman, bird-like and frail, clutching a rosary so hard her knuckles were white. She was muttering something in Latin, or what she thought was Latin. Pious, Arthur thought. A bit self-righteous, judging by the way she kept glancing at the tattooed man with visible distaste. But harmless. Probably just confused.

There was a priest, younger than Arthur expected, staring at his own hands as if they were spiders. His collar was crooked. He looked like he'd been crying. Crisis of faith, Arthur diagnosed with a mental sneer. Pathetic. If you can't hack the big questions, don't take the job.

There was a young man in designer jeans, maybe thirty, tapping his foot and scrolling through a phone that no longer had service. He radiated the specific irritation of someone who'd never had to wait for anything in his life. Atheist, Arthur thought with satisfaction. Tech money, probably. About to have a very rude awakening.

And there was a dog.

A scruffy, brown-and-white mutt of indeterminate breed, lying in the middle of the floor like it owned the place. It looked up at Arthur with soft, patient eyes and gave a hopeful, panting wag of its tail.

Arthur ignored it. *Unsanitary*, he thought. *Why is that here? Probably someone's emotional support animal.* Even in death, standards had declined.

A digital chime—as polite and soulless as a hospital elevator—pinged.

The "NOW SERVING" sign above the single window flashed: 847,291

The tattooed man stood up. Walked to the window with the careful, measured gait of someone who'd spent a lot of time being watched.

Behind the window sat a Clerk. Not an angel. Not a demon. Just... a Clerk. The kind of entity that looked like it had been processing forms since the invention of paperwork and would continue processing forms long after the heat death of the universe. He had the supernatural boredom of a creature who has seen everything and been impressed by none of it.

The Clerk tapped a keyboard with two fingers. "Silas Kane."

The tattooed man nodded once.

"Crime: Murder, first degree. Victim: Raymond Booker, age 34. Method: blunt force trauma. Oakland, California, March 14th, 1987."

Arthur leaned forward, vindicated. Called it.

"Confessed: Yes. Trial: Waived. Sentence: 15 years to life, California State Prison. Time served: 15 years, 4 months, 11 days."

Silas just stood there, hands clasped behind his back like he was still in prison.

"Repentance." The Clerk tapped a key. "Verified."

Arthur frowned. Verified? What did that mean?

"Destination," the Clerk said, picking up a stamp.

Here it comes, Arthur thought. The express elevator down.

THUD.

"Heaven."

Arthur Blackwell stood up so fast his chair scraped against the linoleum. "WHAT?!"

The entire room turned to look at him.

The Clerk didn't even lift his head. "Sir, please take your seat until your number is called."

"That man is a MURDERER!" Arthur sputtered, his face going purple. "He just... you just said... there is no possible way he is permitted to—"

"He confessed," the Clerk said, not unkindly. "He served his time. He demonstrated genuine remorse. The debt was paid."

"Paid?! A man is DEAD!"

"Yes. And Mr. Kane spent 5,475 consecutive days thinking about it." The Clerk stamped another form. "Please return to the main waiting area, Mr. Kane. Your door will open when processing is complete."

Silas turned and walked back to the waiting room. Sat down in the same chair.

Arthur stared at him, mouth working soundlessly.

The dog got up, stretched, and trotted over to Silas. Put its head on his knee.

Silas scratched behind its ears. "Hey, buddy."

The dog's tail wagged.

"This is OBSCENE!" Arthur roared. "This is a MOCKERY of—"

The digital chime pinged.

Now serving: 847,292.

The old woman, Agnes, stood up, smoothing her dress. She shot one last withering glance at Silas before walking to the window with the bearing of someone who'd been waiting her entire life to be recognized for her virtue.

She reached the window. Smiled.

"Agnes Marie Whitmore."

"Yes." Her voice was thin, reedy, proud.

"Life of devotion. Daily Mass attendance: 99.2% over 40 years. Charity work: consistent. Fasting: observed. Confession: weekly. Sins confessed: 2,847, all venial. Major sins: zero."

Agnes beamed. She glanced back at the room, at Arthur, as if to say, "See? This is how it's done."

"Exemplary," the Clerk continued. "One of the most devout records we've processed this quarter."

Agnes smoothed her hair, preparing for her moment. "However."

Her smile froze.

"Sin category: Judgment. Subcategory: Chronic and pervasive."

Her hand went to her throat.

"Mrs. Patterson, criticized for her immodest hemline, June 1987. Mr. Kowalski, judged for missing Mass due to his mother's funeral, September 1991. The Johnson boy, declared 'destined for Hell' for his tattoos, March 2003. The mailman, condemned as a sinner for working Sundays—to deliver your disability checks, I might add. You spent 87 years deciding who was worthy and who was not."

"I was upholding standards!" Agnes's voice cracked. "Someone has to!"

"Matthew 7:1," the Clerk recited. "'Judge not, lest ye be judged.'"

"But I was judging sinners!"

"So is He." The Clerk picked up a different stamp. Red. "And He's better at it."

THUD.

"Destination: Hell."

Agnes made a sound like all the air had been punched out of her. She staggered backward, her rosary beads clattering to the floor.

"But I... I went to church. Every day. I prayed. I fasted—"

"And you judged. Constantly. Please return to the main waiting area. Your door will open when processing is complete. Next."

Agnes stumbled back to her seat. Collapsed into it. Started crying, quiet and broken.

The priest made a small, wounded sound and started praying faster.

The atheist in the designer jeans whispered, "Holy shit."

Arthur's blood had turned to ice.

Judgment.

The word echoed in his head.

The Priest was openly weeping now.

The digital chime pinged.

Now serving: 847,293.

Arthur's number.

He stood. His legs felt like they belonged to someone else.

He walked to the window. Every eye in the room was on him.

He reached the window. Cleared his throat. Tried to summon the authority that had served him for forty years on the bench.

"See here," he began, and his voice came out stronger than he felt. "I am Judge Arthur Blackwell. I have devoted my entire life to the law. To justice. To order. I was a good man. I served God and my community by separating the wheat from the—"

"Arthur Blackwell," the Clerk interrupted, reading from his screen. "Sentenced 847 people over the course of a forty-year career."

"Yes!" Arthur said, some of his confidence returning. "All guilty. All deserving of their punishments. All—"

"Believed he was serving justice. Correct."

"Indeed. So I assume my—"

"However." The Clerk scrolled. "Sin: Judgment."

Arthur's mouth went dry. "...I beg your pardon?"

"You judged. 847 formal sentences. Thousands more informal judgments. The defendant. The prosecution. The jury. The bailiff. The man who made your coffee. The woman who cleaned your courtroom. You judged everyone. You relished it. You slept soundly every night, secure in the belief that your judgment was not only correct but righteous."

"It was my JOB!" Arthur's voice cracked. "I was upholding the LAW! Without judgment, there is no order! There is no justice! There is only—"

"Not," the Clerk said, picking up the red stamp, "your call."

He raised it.

"No... wait! You can't! I'm a good person! I served society! I protected the innocent! I punished the guilty! I—"

THUD.

"Destination: Hell."

The word landed and turned the air in Arthur's lungs into a jelly. Or, at least, it felt that way.

"WHAT?!" Arthur slammed his hands on the counter. "This is—this is INSANE! I upheld the LAW! That murderer gets HEAVEN and I get HELL?!"

"He confessed and repented. You judged and felt righteous. There's a difference."

"DIFFERENCE?! I was APPOINTED by the STATE to—"

"By the state. Not by God." The Clerk stamped another form. "Please return to the main waiting area. Your door will open when processing is complete."

"I demand to speak to a supervisor! I demand an appeal! This is a travesty of—"

"Form 7734. Processing time: eternity. Also, filing an appeal counts as questioning divine judgment, which is itself a sin, so you'd be re-sentenced to Hell. Again. Would you like to proceed?"

Arthur's mouth opened. Closed. Opened again.

Nothing came out.

"Thought not. Return to waiting area. Next."

Arthur turned. Walked back to his seat on legs that no longer felt like they could support him.

He sat down.

The dog trotted over. Looked up at him with those patient, brown eyes. Tail wagging gently.

The dog licked his hand.

Arthur flinched. Pulled it away.

"No," he muttered. "Go away."

The dog tilted its head. Sat there for another moment. Then, when Arthur didn't reach out, padded away.

Across the room, Silas watched this exchange. Said nothing.

The atheist in the designer jeans was staring at Arthur with something between horror and fascination.

The priest had stopped praying and was now just... staring at his hands.

Arthur sat there, numb, as the reality settled over him like a shroud.

He was going to Hell.

Not for cruelty.

Not for corruption.

Not for any of the sins he'd spent forty years punishing in others.

For judgment.

For the one thing he'd believed was his sacred duty.

The digital chime pinged.

Now serving: 847,294.

A thin man with a leather collar stood up and walked to the window.

Episode 2

The Murderer

S ilas Kane had been dead for approximately four minutes when he realized Hell was going to be a lot more boring than he'd expected.

The waiting room smelled like every DMV he'd ever been forced to endure: industrial cleaner, burnt coffee, and the faint electrical tang of fluorescent lights on their last legs. He'd taken his number—847,291—and sat down in a chair that seemed specifically designed to punish the human spine.

He didn't mind waiting. He'd done fifteen years in Pelican Bay. Waiting was a skill he'd mastered somewhere between year three and the heat death of hope.

The old judge—Blackwell, his brain supplied helpfully—was pacing like a caged animal. The man kept standing up, sitting down, muttering calculations under his breath. Judging everyone in sight. Silas recognized the type. He'd been sentenced by that type.

There was a priest in the corner who looked like he'd swallowed his own Bible and was having buyer's remorse. A young guy in designer jeans scrolling through a phone that no longer had service, which seemed to be causing him physical pain. An old woman clutching rosary beads like they were stock certificates.

And a dog.

Brown and white. Scruffy. The kind of mutt you'd see outside a 7-Eleven, tail wagging at strangers, operating on pure, weaponized optimism.

The dog walked over, sniffed Silas's hand, then sat. Tail thumping.

Silas scratched behind its ears. "You get a raw deal too, buddy?"

The dog's tail accelerated. Silas took that as a yes.

The digital chime pinged.

NOW SERVING: 847,291.

Silas stood. Walked to the window.

The Clerk looked like God's accountant after a double shift and three divorces: exhausted, ancient, and so far beyond giving a shit that he'd achieved a kind of zen.

"Silas Kane."

"That's me."

The Clerk tapped his keyboard with the enthusiasm of a man filing his own death certificate. "Crime: Murder, first degree. Victim: Raymond Booker, age 34. Method: blunt force trauma with a tire iron. Location: Oakland, California. Date: March 14th, 1987."

Silas nodded. He remembered. Ray-Ray. Owed him money. Pulled a knife. Silas had been faster. The wet sound. The way Ray-Ray's eyes went from furious to empty in less than a second.

He'd turned himself in six hours later.

"Confessed: Yes. Trial waived. Sentence: 15 years to life, California State Prison. Time served: 15 years, 4 months, 11 days. Good behavior: Consistent. Letters of apology written: 847."

"Sounds about right."

"Repentance." The Clerk tapped another key. Paused. Tapped again. "Verified."

That word landed like a brick through a window.

Silas had spent five years trying to convince himself he wasn't sorry. That Ray-Ray had it coming. That the world was kill-or-be-killed and Silas had simply won the math.

By year six, the lie stopped working.

By year ten, sleep became a luxury he could no longer afford.

By year fifteen, he'd written 847 letters. One to Ray-Ray's mother. To his sister. To his daughter. To everyone Ray-Ray had ever mattered to, tracked down through prison library computers and sheer obsessive penance. Most went unanswered. Three came back. One told him to rot. One forgave him. One said forgiveness wasn't theirs to give, but thanks for asking.

He still didn't know which one hurt more.

"Destination." The Clerk picked up the stamp.

Silas exhaled. He'd made peace with Hell. He deserved it. You took a life, you paid the price. Fifteen years in Pelican Bay hadn't been enough. It would never be enough.

The stamp came down.

THUD.

"Heaven."

Silas blinked. "Come again?"

"Heaven. Please return to the main waiting area. Your door will open when processing is complete."

"Wait. Hold on. I murdered a man."

"Yes."

"With a tire iron."

"Noted."

"I caved in his skull. There was... there was a lot of blood."

The Clerk looked up with the dead-eyed patience of customer service on its 10,000th year. "You confessed. You served your time. You demonstrated genuine remorse. You attempted restitution. The debt is paid. Heaven. Main waiting area. Next."

Behind him, a chair scraped.

Then: "WHAT?!"

Silas turned.

Judge Blackwell was on his feet, face the color of a medical emergency, pointing at Silas like he was Exhibit A in the trial of the century.

"That man is a MURDERER!" Blackwell roared. "I sentenced him myself! Fifteen years! He took a LIFE!"

The Clerk didn't even blink. "And he gave fifteen years. Plus interest. The account is settled."

"Settled?! A man is DEAD!"

"Correct. And Mr. Kane has spent 5,475 consecutive days thinking about it. He wrote 847 letters. He asked for punishment. He wanted to be held accountable. The math checks out."

"This is INSANE!"

"This is divine law. Please sit down, sir, or I will have you removed."

"Removed?! By whom?!"

The Clerk pressed a button. Somewhere in the walls, something mechanical and vaguely ominous groaned to life.

Blackwell sat.

Silas looked at the Clerk. "Can I just—quick question."

"Briefly."

"Did I deserve Heaven?"

The Clerk tilted his head, the first glimmer of something almost human crossing his face. "That's not the question the system asks."

"What's the question?"

"Did you pay what you owed."

Silas thought about that. Thought about Ray-Ray. About his mother, who'd written back and said, I don't forgive you. But I believe you're sorry. And maybe that matters.

"Yeah," Silas said quietly. "I guess I did."

"Then we're done here. Main waiting area. Next."

Silas walked back to the waiting room. Every eye followed him.

He sat down. The dog immediately trotted over and put his head on Silas's knee.

Judge Blackwell was staring at him with the kind of hatred usually reserved for appeals courts.

Silas scratched the dog's ears. "Nice to see you again, Your Honor."

Blackwell's mouth opened. Closed. Opened again. "This is obscene."

"You sentenced me to fifteen years. I did fifteen years. System says we're square."

"The system is broken."

Silas looked at him. Really looked. The man was vibrating with self-righteousness. "You built the system, Your Honor. You and 10,000 judges just like you. Don't get mad now that you're on the other side of the bench."

"I upheld the LAW!"

"So did I. I broke it. I confessed. I paid. That's the deal, right? Or does the deal only work when you're the one holding the gavel?"

Blackwell opened his mouth to respond—

The digital chime pinged.

Now serving: 847,292.

The old woman—Agnes—stood up, smoothing her dress, clutching her rosary like a backstage pass to the VIP lounge.

She walked to the window.

Silas leaned back in his chair. The dog yawned and settled at his feet.

Across the room, the atheist muttered, "This is so fucked up."

The priest, pale and sweating, nodded in silent agreement.

Silas closed his eyes.

Fifteen years, he'd waited for this.

And somehow, it still didn't feel like enough.
The dog's tail thumped twice against the linoleum.
Silas smiled, just a little.
"Yeah, buddy," he whispered. "Me too."

Episode 3

The Saint

Agnes Whitmore had lived 87 years without sin.

Well. Without major sin. She'd been very clear about that distinction to Father Benjamin every Sunday for the last 40 years. Venial sins, perhaps—everyone had those, it was human nature—but nothing mortal. Nothing that would jeopardize her standing.

She'd kept meticulous records. Attended Mass daily. Volunteered at the soup kitchen every Thursday (though she made sure to stand upwind of the homeless, for hygiene reasons). She'd donated 10% of her pension to the church, and had the receipts to prove it, organized by year in a three-ring binder she'd brought with her to the afterlife.

She clutched it now as she approached the window, along with her rosary.

The Clerk looked like he'd been doing this job since the invention of bureaucracy and had long ago accepted that humanity would never improve.

"Agnes Marie Whitmore."

"That's correct." She set the binder on the counter. "I've prepared documentation. Tax receipts, volunteer hours, a letter of recommendation from my priest—"

"Not necessary."

"Oh." She pulled the binder back, mildly offended. "Well. I thought it might expedite—"

"Agnes," the Clerk interrupted, reading from his screen. "Life of devotion. Daily Mass attendance: 99 .2% over 40 years. Charity work: consistent. Fasting: observed. Confession: weekly. Sins confessed: 2,847, all venial. Major sins: zero."

Agnes smiled. Finally. Validation. She'd earned this.

"Exemplary," the Clerk continued. "One of the most devout records we've processed this quarter."

Agnes smoothed her dress, preparing for her entrance. She wondered if there'd be a choir. She hoped there'd be a choir. She'd always loved hymns. Particularly the ones about judgment.

"However."

Agnes's smile froze.

"Sin category: Judgment. Subcategory: Chronic and pervasive."

Her mouth opened. Nothing came out.

The Clerk scrolled. "Let's see. Mrs. Patterson, criticized for her immodest hemline, June 1987. Mr. Kowalski, judged for missing Mass due to his mother's funeral, September 1991. The Johnson boy, declared 'destined for Hell' for his tattoos, March 2003. The mailman, condemned as a sinner for working Sundays—"

"He was working Sundays!" Agnes protested, finding her voice. "It's the Sabbath! It's written!"

"He was delivering your disability checks," the Clerk said flatly.

"That's—that's different—"

"Is it?" The Clerk looked up. "You judged your neighbors. Your priest. The grocery store clerk who smiled too much—you decided she was 'false.' The children in the park who were too loud—'poorly raised.' The woman at the soup kitchen who took two rolls—'greedy.' You spent 87 years deciding who was worthy and who was not."

"I was upholding standards!" Agnes's voice cracked. "Someone has to! If we don't judge sin, how do we know what's righteous?!"

"Matthew, chapter 7, verse 1," the Clerk recited. "'Judge not, lest ye be judged.'"

"But I was judging sinners!"

"So is He." The Clerk picked up the stamp. "And He's better at it."

Agnes grabbed the edge of the counter. "No. No, you don't understand. I lived a good life. I never—I was faithful—"

"You were judgmental."

"I was discerning!"

"Same thing." The stamp hovered. "Mrs. Whitmore, you spent 87 years convinced you knew who deserved Heaven and who didn't. You looked at the homeless man at the soup kitchen and thought, If he'd just tried harder. You looked at the mailman and thought, He's choosing money over God. You looked at everyone and decided you were better. Holier. More deserving."

"I was!" The word came out as a shriek. "I did everything right!"

"You did," the Clerk agreed. "Except the most important thing."

"Which was?!"

"Love thy neighbor." He stamped the form.

THUD.

"Destination: Hell. Return to the main waiting area. Your door will open when processing is complete."

Agnes stood frozen, her face the color of old parchment.

"But I—I went to church. Every day. I prayed. I fasted."

"And you judged. Constantly. Next."

"This is a mistake." Her voice was small now, childlike. "There's been a mistake. I'm—I'm Agnes Whitmore. I'm a good person."

"You're a judgmental person," the Clerk corrected. "There's a difference. Main waiting area. Now."

Agnes stumbled backward. Her three-ring binder slipped from her hands, receipts scattering across the linoleum like damning evidence at a trial.

She turned.

The waiting room stared back at her.

The murderer—the murderer!—was sitting there, petting that filthy dog, looking almost... peaceful.

The judge was glaring at her with something that might have been sympathy, or schadenfreude. Probably both.

The atheist in the designer jeans smirked. "Welcome to the club, grandma."

Agnes's knees buckled.

She didn't quite faint, but it was close. She sank into a chair, rosary beads clicking through her trembling fingers like an abacus calculating her losses.

The dog—that dog—wandered over, tail wagging.

Agnes flinched. "Get away from me. Unclean."

The dog sat. Tilted his head. Kept wagging.

Judge Blackwell laughed. It was a bitter, ugly sound. "Unclean. That's rich. Coming from someone headed to Hell."

Agnes's head snapped up. "You're going to Hell too!"

"I know!" Blackwell barked. "Because apparently spending 40 years upholding the law counts as judging! Just like spending 87 years being a sanctimonious, self-righteous—"

"I was devout!"

"You were insufferable!" The atheist stood up. "Lady, I didn't even believe in this shit, and I got into Heaven. You spent your whole life kissing God's ass and you still got sent downstairs. You know what that means?"

Agnes stared at him, shaking.

"It means you sucked at it."

Silas, still petting the dog, spoke quietly. "Maybe it wasn't about how much you prayed. Maybe it was about how you treated people."

Agnes whirled on him. "And you would know? You murdered someone!"

"Yeah." Silas nodded. "I did. And I've spent fifteen years wishing I hadn't. How long have you spent wishing you'd been kinder?"

The words hit like a slap.

Agnes opened her mouth. Closed it.

The dog licked her hand.

She yanked it away.

Across the room, the priest made a small, wounded sound. He looked like he might be sick.

The digital chime pinged.

Now serving: 847,293.

Judge Blackwell stood, pale and furious. "That's me. Again."

He walked to the window.

Agnes sat in her chair, clutching her rosary, staring at the scattered receipts on the floor.

Proof of her devotion.

Evidence of her damnation.

The dog lay down at her feet and sighed.

Episode 4

The Masochist

J udge Blackwell marched to the window, jaw set, ready for round two.

The Clerk didn't even look up. "You've already been processed."

"Then why did you call my number?!"

The Clerk tapped his keyboard with the energy of a man who'd stopped caring sometime during the Crusades. "System glitch. You're still in queue for... let's see... appeals processing."

Blackwell's eyes lit up. "I can appeal?!"

"You can file an appeal. Form 7734. Processing time: eternity." The Clerk finally looked up. "Also, filing an appeal counts as questioning divine judgment, which is itself a sin. You'll be re-sentenced to Hell. Again. Would you like to proceed?"

Blackwell's mouth worked soundlessly.

"Thought not. Return to waiting area."

"But—"

"Next."

Blackwell stood there, vibrating with impotent rage, then turned and shuffled back to his seat like a man who'd just lost an argument with a parking meter.

The chime pinged again.

Now serving: 847,294.

A man stood up.

He was thin, pale, maybe forty. Black turtleneck. Leather collar with a small silver ring. His eyes held the specific brightness of someone who'd spent a lifetime chasing something just out of reach.

He walked to the window like a pilgrim approaching a shrine.

Agnes clutched her rosary tighter. "Is that—is he wearing a collar?"

The atheist snorted. "Yeah. And not the priest kind."

The man reached the window. Took a breath. Smiled. "Sebastian Caine."

The Clerk read from his screen, voice flat as week-old communion bread. "Occupation: financial analyst. Hobbies: extensive. Personal life: complicated. Sins: numerous and varied."

Sebastian nodded eagerly. "Yes. All documented. I kept journals."

"You... kept journals of your sins."

"Meticulous ones. Categorized by severity. Cross-referenced with relevant scripture." Sebastian leaned forward. "I assume that helps with processing?"

The Clerk stared at him. "It's a first."

"I tried to be thorough. I know what I did. I know what I deserve." Sebastian's voice dropped to something almost reverent. "I'm ready."

"Ready for...?"

"Hell." The word came out like a prayer. "I've spent my entire adult life earning it. Every cruelty. Every lie. Every moment of selfishness. I want this. I need this. It's the only thing that makes sense."

The Clerk blinked. Once. Slowly. "You... want to go to Hell."

"Desperately."

"Why."

Sebastian spread his hands like he was explaining something obvious. "Because I deserve it. Because punishment gives meaning to sin. Because—" His voice cracked slightly. "Because if there's no Hell for people like me, then nothing matters. Do you understand? I need there to be consequences. I need the universe to have rules."

The Clerk looked at him for a long moment.

"Interesting."

He typed. Scrolled. Typed some more.

Sebastian waited, practically vibrating with anticipation.

"Confession of sins: comprehensive. Self-awareness: exceptional. Desire for punishment: pathological." The Clerk paused. "Hmm."

"Hmm?" Sebastian's voice went up an octave. "What does 'hmm' mean?"

"Repentance."

"I don't repent! That's the point! I knew what I was doing! I chose it!"

"But you confessed."

"Because I'm honest about being terrible!"

"Confession implies remorse."

"No it doesn't! Confession is just... accurate self-reporting!"

The Clerk tapped his keyboard. "System interprets comprehensive confession as evidence of genuine self-examination. Self-examination implies capacity for growth. Capacity for growth implies—"

"No." Sebastian's hands slammed on the counter. "No, no, no. I do not have capacity for growth. I'm broken. Fundamentally. Irreparably. That's the whole point."

"The system disagrees." The Clerk picked up the stamp.

Sebastian's eyes went wide. "Wait. What are you—"

THUD.

"Destination: Heaven."

The word hit Sebastian like a physical blow. He staggered backward.

"No."

"Please return to main waiting area. Your door will open when—"

"NO!" Sebastian's voice cracked. "You can't! I earned Hell! I worked for it! Do you know how much effort I put into being irredeemable?!"

"Considerable, apparently. Next."

"I want Hell! I need Hell! Heaven is—it's—" Sebastian's breath came in short gasps. "How can I exist in Heaven knowing what I am? Knowing what I did? It would be torture!"

The Clerk looked up. Something almost like interest flickered across his face.

"Yes," he said simply. "It would."

Sebastian's face went through several expressions in rapid succession: confusion, realization, horror, and finally, a kind of broken understanding.

"Oh," he whispered. "Oh, you bastards."

"Main waiting area. Now."

Sebastian stumbled back to the waiting room on legs that didn't quite work. He collapsed into a chair, face in his hands, breathing like he'd just run a marathon.

Agnes shot to her feet, rosary clutched in white-knuckled fists.

"This is obscene!" Her voice cracked with righteous fury. "A man who wants damnation gets Heaven?! A murderer gets Heaven! I spend 87 years in service to God and I get Hell?! Where is the justice?!"

She gestured wildly, and the heavy crucifix on her rosary swung out in a wide arc.

CRACK.

It caught Sebastian across the cheek.

Sebastian gasped.

His back arched.

His eyes rolled back slightly.

A low, involuntary moan escaped his lips.

The room went silent.

Everyone stared.

"Oh my God," the atheist whispered. "Did he just—"

"Yes," Sebastian breathed, eyes still closed, cheeks flushed. "Yes. Yes, I did." He opened his eyes, looked at Agnes with something disturbingly close to gratitude. "Thank you. Could you—could you do that again?"

Agnes dropped the rosary like it had burst into flames. "You—you're a—a pervert!"

"Masochist," Sebastian corrected, still catching his breath. "Technically. And yes. Obviously." He touched his cheek where the crucifix had hit. "Did the collar not give it away?"

Blackwell made a strangled sound. "This is a waiting room for the afterlife and you're—you're enjoying—"

"Pain," Sebastian finished flatly. "Yes. I'm wired for it. I've spent my entire life seeking it because it's the only thing that feels real. And now—" His voice broke. "Now they're sending me to Heaven. Eternal comfort. Eternal peace. Eternal gentleness." He looked at Agnes, then at the rosary on the floor. "Do you understand? They're sending me to the one place where I'll never feel that again. Ever. That's my Hell."

Silas, still sitting with the dog, spoke quietly. "You wanted to be punished."

"I needed to be punished," Sebastian said. "I need pain to feel alive. I need consequences to make sense of my choices. And Heaven is—" He laughed, high and broken. "Heaven is a place where nothing ever hurts. Where everything is soft and kind and gentle." His hands were shaking. "I'll be in agony for eternity."

The atheist rubbed his face. "Man, that is fucked up."

"I know."

The dog trotted over, tail wagging, and gently placed its head on Sebastian's knee.

Sebastian looked down at it. At the soft brown eyes. The gentle, unconditional affection radiating from every inch of its scruffy body.

"Even you," he whispered. "Even you're too kind."

The dog licked his hand.

Sebastian started crying. Not the dramatic tears of Agnes or the rage-tears of Blackwell. Just quiet, defeated sobbing.

The priest in the corner looked like he might be sick. His hands were clasped so tightly his knuckles had gone white.

Silas watched Sebastian for a long moment. "I get it," he said finally.

Everyone looked at him.

"The needing to be punished part. Thinking you don't deserve forgiveness." Silas scratched the dog's ears. "I spent fifteen years thinking the same thing. That I didn't deserve Heaven. That I was too broken."

"You are broken," Sebastian said without heat. "We both are."

"Yeah." Silas nodded. "But maybe that's not the point."

"Then what is the point?"

Silas looked at the dog, then at Sebastian. "I don't know yet. But I think—" He paused. "I think maybe it's not about what we deserve. Maybe it's about something else."

Blackwell snorted. "Platitudes. Wonderful. Meanwhile, I upheld the law for forty years and I'm going to Hell alongside a murderer and a—a—" He gestured at Sebastian. "Whatever he is!"

"The system's ironic," the atheist said. "That's what it is. The people who tried hardest to be good get Hell. The people who know they're shit get Heaven. It's like God's playing a joke."

"Or," the priest said, voice barely audible, "it's not about being good. It's about something we don't understand yet."

Everyone looked at him.

He was staring at his hands like they belonged to someone else.

The digital chime pinged.

Now SERVING: 847,295.

The priest stood slowly, like he was walking to his own execution.

His hands were shaking.

He walked to the window.

Sebastian, still crying quietly, looked at Agnes's rosary on the floor.

The atheist noticed. "Don't even think about it."

"I wasn't," Sebastian lied.

The dog stayed at his knee, tail thumping gently against the linoleum.

Sebastian petted it with trembling hands. "You're a good dog," he whispered. "Even if you're my eternal punishment."

The dog's tail wagged harder.

Episode 5

The Priest

Father Benjamin Haas stood. The movement felt heavy, as if he were trying to walk through wet cement.

For forty years, he had been the authority. He was the one who explained the afterlife. He was the one who charted the map to Heaven and warned of the paths to Hell. He had counseled Agnes on her piety. He had heard confessions from men just like Silas. He had, on three occasions, given last rites to men Judge Blackwell had sentenced to death.

He knew this system. He had taught this system.

And he had just watched it fail, spectacularly, in every conceivable way.

The atheist leaned over to Silas. "Ten bucks says the priest gets Hell."

"I'm not taking that bet," Silas muttered. "At this point, I think the Pope would get Hell."

"The Pope probably did get Hell," Sebastian added, still red-eyed. "And he's probably thrilled about it."

Father Benjamin reached the window. The Clerk looked at him with the same expression he'd given everyone else: absolute, cosmic boredom.

"Father Benjamin Haas."

"Yes." The word came out like sandpaper.

"Ordained: 1983. Vow of poverty: observed. Vow of chastity: observed." The Clerk paused. "Well. Mostly observed."

Benjamin flushed. "That was one time! And we didn't—it was just—"

"Relax. It's not on the list." The Clerk scrolled. "Devotion: absolute. Sermons given: 2,080. Confessions heard: 34,712."

Benjamin nodded. The numbers of his life, quantified.

"And in every single sermon," the Clerk continued flatly, "you preached the Law. The rules. The fire. The judgment."

"I preached the Word of God!" Benjamin's voice cracked. "I preached what was written! Sin must be confronted!"

"Must it?" The Clerk's finger stopped on the screen. "Let's look at those confessions. 34,712 souls who trusted you as their shepherd. Their conduit to grace."

The atheist whispered to Silas: "Oh, this is gonna be bad."

"March 1994. A woman confesses her husband beats her. She asks if she has God's permission to leave."

Benjamin's blood turned to ice. He remembered. Elara Sanchez. Dark eyes. Trembling hands. The bruise on her wrist she kept trying to hide with her sleeve.

"I... I told her to pray. That marriage was a sacred vow. That she must work to save his soul."

"You told her it was her duty to endure," the Clerk corrected. "You judged her desire for safety as impatience. As a failure of faith. She stayed. He broke her jaw two weeks later. She lost the child she was carrying."

The atheist made a sound like he'd been punched.

Agnes gasped, hand over her mouth.

"I didn't know—" Benjamin started.

"You didn't ask," the Clerk said. "You had a wounded sheep in front of you, and you gave her a stone wrapped in scripture." He scrolled. "Next. 2005. A young man, seventeen years old, confesses he is gay. He's terrified. Suicidal. He asks for guidance. For comfort."

Benjamin's hands were shaking. "I... I told him to pray for deliverance. That the act was a mortal sin. That he must resist his—"

"He killed himself four days later," the Clerk interrupted. "Drove his father's car into a tree at seventy miles an hour. He left a note. It said, 'I guess God hates me.'"

"Oh fuck," the atheist breathed.

"NO!" Benjamin slammed his hand on the counter, the first real passion he'd shown. "That is not my sin! I gave him the Church's teaching! I gave him the Law! I didn't tell him to—"

"Your job," the Clerk interrupted, and his voice dropped to something cold and vast, "was to love. Your job was to be the shepherd. To comfort the afflicted. To bind up the broken. You heard 34,712 confessions, and in every single one, you chose to be a judge. You listened for the sin instead of the suffering."

"I thought... I thought I was doing God's work."

The Clerk picked up the stamp. "You were doing Agnes's work. You were doing the Judge's work. You were so terrified of sin that you forgot to see the sinner. You were so obsessed with the rules that you forgot the reason."

"But I believed," Benjamin whispered. "I gave up everything."

"Yes," the Clerk said. "You did."

THUD.

"And it was for nothing. Destination: Hell."

Silence.

Then—

"HAH!" Judge Blackwell shot to his feet, pointing at the Priest. "A PRIEST! Even the CLERGY get Hell for judging! This is—this is validating! Don't you see? If priests are getting damned, then clearly the system is fundamentally—"

The Clerk's voice crackled over the intercom. "Your appeal was denied."

Blackwell froze. "I didn't even file it yet!"

"Pre-emptively denied. We saw it coming. Return to waiting area."

"But I—"

"Now."

Blackwell sat down, deflated.

Agnes clutched her rosary. "Father Benjamin, I'm so—"

"Don't," he said quietly, walking back to his seat. "Just... don't."

He collapsed into his chair, staring at nothing. His hands—the hands that had blessed bread, anointed the sick, pushed away a desperate boy—hung limp at his sides.

He felt hollow. Scooped out. Forty years of devotion, and it had all been performance. Theater. He'd been so busy being righteous that he'd forgotten to be kind.

After a long, uncomfortable silence, Sebastian cleared his throat.

"Hey. Father."

Benjamin didn't look up. "What."

"I'll trade you."

That got Benjamin's attention. He looked up, confused. "What?"

"I got Heaven. You got Hell. Let's switch. I'm serious. Please. I'm begging you."

Benjamin stared at him. "That's... that's not how this works."

"Have you asked?" Sebastian looked toward the Clerk's window. "Excuse me! Is there a destination swap option?"

"No," the Clerk said without looking up.

"What if I pay a processing fee?"

"There is no fee structure for destination exchanges."

"What if I file a formal request?"

"Form 666-R. Processing time: eternity. Also, requesting Hell counts as ingratitude for your assigned Heaven, which is itself a sin of pride, so you'd be re-sentenced to Heaven. Again."

Sebastian slumped. "Of course. Of course."

Benjamin looked at him, this strange, broken man. "You... you actually want my Hell?"

"More than anything."

"Then you're crazier than I am."

"Probably," Sebastian agreed. "But at least I'm self-aware about it."

The dog, who'd been sitting quietly by Silas, stood up. It stretched, yawned, and trotted over to Father Benjamin.

It sat at his feet. Looked up at him with soft, brown, uncomplicated eyes. Its tail gave a gentle thump against the linoleum.

This was it. A creature of pure, simple love. No theology. No judgment. No tests.

Just... kindness.

Benjamin looked at the dog.

He looked at his hands.

The hands that had failed Elara. The hands that had failed that boy. The hands that had, for forty years, dispensed judgment disguised as grace.

The hands that were damned.

He couldn't. He was unclean. He was a fraud. He would... taint it.

Slowly, carefully, Father Benjamin pulled his hand back.

"I can't," he whispered. "I'm sorry. I can't."

The dog whimpered once, confused.

Then it padded away.

Silas, who'd been watching the whole thing, stared at Benjamin like he'd just kicked a puppy.

"Did you just... refuse to pet the dog?"

Benjamin didn't answer.

"Man, it's a dog. Dogs don't give a shit about 'worthy.' They just want—"

"I can't," Benjamin said, voice breaking.

Silas shook his head. "You priests. Always making everything complicated." He scratched the dog's ears as it returned to him. "Come here, buddy. He doesn't deserve you anyway."

The dog's tail wagged.

Benjamin looked at Silas—the murderer—showing more grace than he ever had.

"You're right," he said quietly. "I don't."

"That wasn't a compliment," Silas muttered.

Agnes, after a long moment, stood. She walked over to Benjamin, clutching her rosary like a life preserver.

"Father Benjamin," she said softly.

"Don't."

"We can pray together. We can—"

"YOU'RE GOING TO HELL TOO, AGNES!" Benjamin's voice cracked like a whip. "We're in the same boat! Don't you understand?"

Agnes flinched. "I... I was just trying to help."

"So was I!" Benjamin laughed, bitter and broken. "So was I. That's the problem. We both spent our lives judging people. We both thought we were righteous. We were both wrong."

Agnes, pale, slowly sat back down.

Blackwell muttered, "Well, this is fucking depressing."

The atheist nodded. "Yeah. This got dark fast."

"At least he's not a molester," Sebastian offered weakly.

Everyone turned to look at him.

"What? I'm just saying, it could be worse. He could've been—you know—actually one of those priests. The kid-touching kind." Sebastian shrugged. "Silver lining?"

"That's not a silver lining," the atheist said. "That's just... not being a monster."

"In this room?" Sebastian gestured around. "I'll take what I can get."

Silas snorted despite himself.

Even Benjamin, hollow as he was, made a sound that might have been a laugh. Or a sob. Hard to tell.

The digital chime pinged.

Now serving: 847,296.

The atheist stood up slowly, brushing off his designer jeans.

"Well," he said to no one in particular. "This ought to be interesting."

He looked at the room. The damned judge. The damned saint. The damned priest. The murderer going to Heaven. The masochist being tortured with mercy.

"At least I already didn't believe in any of this shit," he muttered.

He walked to the window.

Behind him, Father Benjamin sat with his face in his hands, and for the first time in forty years, he had absolutely no idea what to pray for.

The dog, tired of the heavy atmosphere, lay down in the middle of the room and sighed deeply.

Everyone, for just a moment, envied the dog.

Episode 6

The Atheist

Marcus Lambert walked to the window like a man approaching a punchline he'd already figured out.

He was thirty-two. Tech startup money. Designer everything. He'd died in a Tesla that decided lane-assist was more of a suggestion than a rule. One minute he was answering emails at 80 mph, the next he was here, waiting in God's DMV with a bunch of people having existential crises.

He'd spent the last hour watching the system systematically demolish every religious person in the room while rewarding the guy who murdered someone and tormenting the guy who wanted to be tortured.

If this was divine justice, God had a fucked-up sense of humor.

The Clerk looked up. "Marcus Lambert."

"That's me."

"Occupation: software engineer, venture capital backed startup. Net worth at time of death: 4.2 million. Charitable giving: minimal. Religious affiliation: none."

"Atheist," Marcus clarified. "Capital A. Card-carrying member of the 'I'll believe it when I see it' club." He gestured around the waiting room. "Though I gotta say, this is not what I expected to see."

"Few people do. Belief system: materialist rationalism. Church attendance: zero. Prayer: zero. Acknowledged existence of higher power: zero."

"Correct on all counts."

"However." The Clerk scrolled. "Acts of kindness: significant. Helped elderly neighbor with groceries every week for four years, no expectation of recognition. Donated bone marrow to stranger, anonymous registry. Spent three months teaching coding to underprivileged kids, unpaid. Gave your Tesla to your sister when her car died—"

"Wait, wait." Marcus held up a hand. "My Tesla killed me."

"Technically your sister's now. She sold it."

"Smart woman."

"Never posted about charitable acts on social media. Never sought credit. Never used altruism as social currency." The Clerk looked up. "Why?"

Marcus shrugged. "Because people needed help? I don't know, man. It's not complicated. You see someone struggling, you help. That's just... being a decent human."

"Without expectation of divine reward?"

"I mean, obviously. I didn't think anyone was keeping score."

"We are," the Clerk said. "Always."

Marcus laughed. "Well, shit. If I'd known, I would've helped way more old ladies across the street."

Behind him, Agnes made a small, wounded sound.

The Clerk picked up the stamp.

Marcus tensed. This was it. The cosmic 'gotcha.' The universe's revenge on every smug atheist who ever said 'I told you so' at a funeral.

THUD.

"Destination: Heaven."

Marcus blinked. "...Seriously?"

"Seriously."

"But I didn't believe in any of this." He gestured at the room. "No church. No prayer. No... God stuff."

"Correct."

"I literally spent my entire adult life thinking religion was a collective delusion designed to make people feel better about dying."

"Also correct."

"And I'm going to Heaven? While—" Marcus turned, pointing at Agnes, "—she spent 87 years in church and got Hell?"

"Correct."

Agnes looked like she might faint again.

"That's insane," Marcus said.

"That's divine law," the Clerk replied. "She judged. You didn't. You helped people because you thought it was the right thing to do, not because you wanted a reward. That's the difference."

"But I didn't even believe in you people!"

"Irrelevant." The Clerk stamped a form. "Matthew 25:40. 'As you did it to one of the least of these, you did it to me.' You fed the hungry. Clothed the naked. Visited the sick. You did all of it without ever believing anyone was watching. That counts."

Marcus stood there, completely at a loss.

Judge Blackwell shot to his feet. "This is absurd! He's an ATHEIST! He didn't even try to be good! He just—he just—"

"Helped people," Silas finished quietly. "Without expecting anything back."

"But I upheld the LAW!" Blackwell roared. "I dedicated my life to justice!"

"You dedicated your life to judgment," the Clerk said without looking up. "There's a difference. Mr. Lambert, please return to the main waiting area. Your door will open when processing is complete. Next."

Marcus walked back to the waiting room in a daze.

He sat down.

Everyone stared at him.

"So," Sebastian said after a long pause. "How does it feel to accidentally win the cosmic lottery?"

"Weird," Marcus admitted. "Really, really weird."

"You didn't even try," Agnes whispered, and there was something close to fury in her voice. "You didn't pray. You didn't worship. You didn't sacrifice."

"I gave bone marrow," Marcus offered. "That hurt like a bitch."

"That's not what I—"

"I know what you mean." Marcus looked at her. "And yeah, you're right. I didn't try. I just... lived. Tried not to be an asshole. Helped when I could. That was it."

"And it was enough," Father Benjamin said, and his voice was hollow. "All the prayers, all the fasting, all the belief—none of it mattered. Just... basic human decency."

"Apparently," Marcus said.

Blackwell laughed. It was an ugly, broken sound. "So the secret to Heaven is to not give a shit about Heaven. Perfect. Absolutely perfect."

"I think," Silas said slowly, scratching the dog's ears, "it's more that the secret is to not judge. Not to think you're better. Not to—"

"Not to care about the rules," Marcus finished. "Yeah. I'm getting that." He looked at the Priest. "No offense, Father, but your system was kind of fucked."

"It wasn't my system," Benjamin said quietly.

"You sure about that? Because from where I'm sitting, it looks like you guys made the system. All the rules, all the judgment, all the 'you're going to Hell if you don't do exactly what we say'—that was you. Not—" He gestured vaguely upward. "—whatever's actually running this place."

The Priest had no response.

The dog wandered over to Marcus and put its head on his knee.

Marcus scratched behind its ears automatically. "Hey, buddy. You seem like the only one here who's got it figured out."

The dog's tail wagged.

"What's his name?" Marcus asked.

"We don't know," Silas said. "He just showed up."

"Probably going to Heaven too," Sebastian muttered bitterly. "The dog gets Heaven. I get Heaven. The atheist gets Heaven. Meanwhile—" He gestured at Agnes, Blackwell, and Father Benjamin. "—you three get Hell for trying too hard."

"The system's not broken," Marcus said, still petting the dog. "It's just not what any of you thought it was."

"Then what is it?" Agnes demanded.

Marcus thought about it. About the Clerk's bored face. About Silas getting Heaven for murder. About Sebastian getting Heaven as punishment. About this whole bizarre, bureaucratic nightmare.

"Honestly?" Marcus said. "I think it's checking if you were an asshole. That's it. Did you help people? Cool, Heaven. Did you spend your life judging everyone else? Hell. It's not about belief. It's about behavior."

"That's reductive," Father Benjamin said.

"Maybe. But look around. The guy who killed someone and felt bad about it? Heaven. The guy who helped old ladies with groceries? Heaven. The people who spent their whole lives telling everyone else they were going to Hell?" He looked at Agnes, Blackwell, and Benjamin. "Hell."

No one had a response to that.

The digital chime pinged.

Now serving: 847,297.

Everyone looked around.

A man stood up from the far corner—how had they not noticed him before?

He was wearing traditional clothing. Beard. Late twenties. He'd been sitting quietly, hands folded, the entire time.

He walked to the window with the expression of someone about to collect a prize.

The Clerk looked up. "Rashid Al-Mansour."

"Yes." His voice was calm. Certain.

"Cause of death: suicide bombing. Civilian casualties: 14. Belief: martyrdom guarantees Paradise and 72 virgins."

Rashid nodded, serene. "I sacrificed myself for the cause. I am ready for my reward."

The Clerk typed. Scrolled. Typed some more.

Long silence.

"Well?" Rashid asked, a slight edge creeping into his voice.

"Complicated case. Multiple jurisdictions claiming authority. Heaven argues martyrdom. Hell argues mass murder. The Virgin Allocation Department is... backed up."

"Backed up?"

"Severely. There's been a significant increase in martyrdom claims since the Internet age. Current wait time for processing: approximately 4,000 years."

Rashid's serenity cracked. "Four thousand years?"

"Give or take. Eternity has no timeline, but current projections suggest—"

"Where are my virgins?!"

"Pending allocation. Please return to main waiting area. You'll be notified when processing is complete."

"But I earned them! I died for the cause!"

"Noted. Next."

"This is unacceptable! I demand to speak to—"

"File a complaint. Form 72-V. Processing time: eternity. Next."

Rashid stood there, vibrating with outrage, then walked back to the waiting room and collapsed into his chair, muttering in Arabic.

Marcus leaned over to Silas. "Did that guy just get put on hold for 4,000 years?"

"Yep," Silas said. "Even in the afterlife, customer service sucks."

Sebastian laughed despite himself.

The digital chime pinged again.

NOW SERVING: 847,298.

Everyone looked around again.

Then, from the far corner near a restroom no one had noticed, a man emerged.

Middle-aged. Unremarkable. Thinning hair. Glasses. Cardigan from a thrift store.

He looked nervous.

Very nervous.

He walked toward the window, and everyone in the room felt an immediate, instinctive revulsion.

They didn't know why.

Not yet.

But something about him was wrong.

The dog, still sitting by Marcus, growled.

Low. Deep.

It was the first sound the dog had made that wasn't friendly.

Marcus looked down. "Buddy? You okay?"

The dog's hackles rose.

Sebastian, watching, went very still. "Oh. Oh, this is going to be bad."

The man reached the window.

The Clerk looked up.

"Jonathan Murphy."

Episode 7

The Molester

Jonathan Murphy walked to the window like a man walking to his own execution.

He was fifty-seven. Thinning hair. Glasses held together with tape. A cardigan that had seen better decades. He looked like every middle school math teacher who'd ever existed.

Behind him, the waiting room had gone silent.

Not the comfortable silence of people waiting their turn.

The *wrong* silence.

The kind of silence that happens when everyone's prey-animal instincts start screaming at once.

The dog, sitting by Marcus's feet, went rigid. His ears flattened against his skull.

Marcus looked down. "Buddy? You okay?"

The dog didn't respond. Just stared at the man walking to the window.

Sebastian, watching, whispered to Silas: "The dog knows something."

"Yeah," Silas said quietly. "Animals always know."

Jonathan reached the window. His hands were shaking.

The Clerk looked up. "Jonathan Murphy."

"Yes." The word came out barely audible.

"Crime: Sexual abuse of minors. Victims: 23. Duration: 18 years. Method: grooming, manipulation, positions of trust violated."

The room went from silent to airless.

Agnes made a small sound of horror.

Father Benjamin's face went gray.

Even Rashid, who'd been muttering about virgin allocation, stopped mid-sentence.

Jonathan's voice was thin, reedy. "I... I confessed. To all of it. I turned myself in. I—"

"Confessed: Yes. Trial: Guilty on all counts. Sentence: 20 years, released early. Behavior in prison: Exemplary. Therapy: Completed. Risk assessment at release: Low."

The Clerk scrolled.

"Post-release: Victim restitution program. Funded 18 college scholarships, anonymous. Volunteer work with abuse prevention organizations, 10 years. Letters of apology: All 23 victims contacted. Three restraining orders received. Two letters of... cautious forgiveness. Eighteen non-responses."

Jonathan was crying now. Quiet, broken tears. "I destroyed lives. I know that. I spent 10 years trying to—trying to make—"

"Restitution. Yes. We have the documentation."

Judge Blackwell shot to his feet. "Are you seriously considering—"

"Sit down, sir," the Clerk said without looking up.

"He's a child molester! Twenty-three victims! Eighteen years! There has to be a line somewhere!"

"I'm aware of the crimes. Sit down or you will be removed."

Blackwell sat, vibrating with fury, but his hands gripped the armrests like he was trying to physically restrain himself from standing again.

Silas, sitting nearby, leaned toward Marcus. Whispered: "This is fucked up."

"Yeah," Marcus said quietly.

"But... I mean, he did serve his time. That's the rule, right? Confession plus time equals—"

"Doesn't make it feel any less wrong."

"No," Silas said. "No, it doesn't."

The Clerk tapped his keyboard. "Repentance: Genuine, verified. Trauma caused: Catastrophic, measurable, permanent. Restitution: Significant but insufficient. Question before the system: Can any act of penance balance 23 destroyed childhoods?"

Silence.

"The math," the Clerk continued, "doesn't work."

Jonathan nodded, defeated. "I know."

"However. Confession: Complete. Punishment: Served. Genuine transformation: Documented. Twenty years of penance. The system must weigh—"

"NO." Silas stood up. Silas, who'd gotten Heaven for murder. Silas, who'd been the calmest person in the room this entire time. "No. There's a difference. I killed a man in a fight. One man. One moment. This—" He pointed at Jonathan. "This is systematic. 23 kids. 18 years. That's not a moment of rage. That's a choice. Over and over."

Jonathan didn't defend himself. Just stood there, taking it.

The Clerk looked at Silas. "And yet he served his time. The system—"

Blackwell was on his feet again. "The system is broken! There has to be something that's unforgivable! If not this, then what?!"

"Judge Blackwell, sit down. Final warning."

Blackwell sat, but his jaw was clenched so tight it looked painful.

The Clerk picked up the stamp. Paused. Put it down. Picked it up again.

For the first time, the Clerk looked... uncertain.

"This is a difficult case," he admitted.

Behind them, Sebastian laughed. High, brittle. "Oh, now it's difficult? The murderer was easy. The atheist was easy. But the child molester? That's where you draw the line?"

"There are... complicating factors."

"Like what?" Father Benjamin demanded, voice shaking. "What could possibly complicate this?"

The Clerk looked at Jonathan. "Tell them."

Jonathan closed his eyes. "I was... I was abused. As a child. By my uncle. For six years. I told people. No one believed me. I told my parents. They said I was lying for attention. I told a teacher. She said I was troubled. I told a priest—" He looked at Father Benjamin. "He said I was 'confused about normal affection.'"

Father Benjamin made a wounded sound.

Marcus shook his head but said nothing.

"That doesn't excuse—" Blackwell started.

"I'm not saying it does!" Jonathan's voice cracked. "It doesn't excuse anything! But the question is... if the system failed me, if the adults who should have protected me didn't, if the cycle just... continued..." He looked at the Clerk. "Where does the blame stop?"

The Clerk nodded slowly. "Where does the blame stop. That's the question."

"It stops with him!" Agnes said, voice trembling with rage. "He made the choice! He knew what it felt like! He should have—"

"Should have broken the cycle," Jonathan finished. "I know. And I didn't. And 23 kids paid the price for that failure."

The stamp hovered.

Jonathan looked at the room. At the faces full of disgust, rage, horror.

"I don't want Heaven," he said quietly. "I don't deserve it. Send me to Hell. Please. It's where I belong."

"The Masochist's Gambit," the Clerk said. "Wanting Hell to avoid the guilt of mercy. Noted." He picked up the stamp. "However. The system has rules."

THUD.

"Destination: Heaven."

Blackwell exploded. "WHAT?!"

Agnes screamed. "NO!"

Father Benjamin just stared, mouth open.

Sebastian: "This is insane!"

Marcus sat very still, watching, but said nothing.

Jonathan stood there, stunned. Shaking. "But I—I don't—"

"Return to main waiting area," the Clerk said. "Your door will open when processing is complete."

Jonathan turned, dazed.

That's when she appeared.

A little girl.

Maybe eight years old. Blonde pigtails. Clutching a stuffed rabbit that had seen better days. She wore a sundress with flowers on it.

She materialized near the Heaven door, holding a number ticket: 847,297-A.

She'd been processed earlier. Fast-tracked, probably. Kids usually were.

She was just waiting for her door to open.

She sat down on the floor, cross-legged, humming quietly to herself.

Jonathan saw her.

Froze.

Everyone watched.

His face... changed.

Not overtly. Just a subtle shift in his expression.

A slight smile.

The kind of smile that makes your skin crawl without knowing exactly why.

The dog, still sitting by Marcus, went from rigid to trembling.

A low growl started deep in his chest.

Marcus's hand went to the dog's collar. "Easy. Easy, buddy."

But the growl got louder.

Jonathan looked at the dog.

His smile faded.

"Fuck off, mutt."

He turned back to the girl.

Started walking toward her.

The dog lunged.

Marcus lost his grip on the collar.

The dog crossed the room in three bounds and planted himself between Jonathan and the child.

Hackles up. Teeth bared. Snarling.

Jonathan stopped. "Move."

The dog didn't move.

The little girl looked up, confused. Scared.

Jonathan took another step.

The dog snapped at his leg—warning.

"I said move."

Jonathan reached for the girl—

The dog bit him.

Hard.

Sank teeth into Jonathan's calf.

Jonathan screamed.

Yanked his leg back.

The dog held on for a second, then released.

Jonathan stumbled backward, clutching his bleeding leg.

And then his face twisted.

Pure rage.

"YOU FUCKING PIECE OF SHIT!"

He kicked the dog.

Hard.

The dog yelped and hit the floor, sliding across the linoleum.

The little girl screamed.

Jonathan turned back to her, face red, breathing hard—

Silas was there.

Moved faster than anyone thought possible.

Grabbed Jonathan by the collar, spun him around, slammed him face-first into the wall.

Hard.

"Don't. You. Fucking. Move."

The entire room erupted.

Marcus had already scooped up the little girl, moved her to the far corner, kneeling in front of her. "It's okay. You're safe. He can't hurt you."

Agnes was on her feet, rushing over. "Sweetheart, it's alright. You're safe now."

The girl was crying, clutching her rabbit.

Father Benjamin looked like he might be sick.

Sebastian just stared, wide-eyed.

Even Rashid looked shaken.

Blackwell stood at the window, pounding his fist on the counter. "I told you! I told you there has to be a line!"

The Clerk's voice cut through the chaos like a knife. "Revised verdict."

Everyone froze.

Silas still had Jonathan pinned.

"Subject displayed predatory intent toward minor. Approached despite protective intervention. Dismissed warning. Assaulted defender. Attempted continued approach."

"I didn't DO anything!" Jonathan's voice was muffled against the wall. "I was just going to—"

"Sit near her," the Clerk finished. "Yes. We know. Intent detected. Behavior pattern consistent with pre-incarceration actions. Forty years of rehabilitation: Invalidated."

"I didn't TOUCH her!"

"You intended to. You smiled. Predatory affect recognized. You dismissed protective barrier. You assaulted innocent creature defending vulnerable target." The Clerk picked up a different stamp. Red. "Intent is sufficient."

THUD.

"Destination: Hell. Immediate processing."

Two massive figures materialized—guards, angels, something—and pulled Jonathan from Silas's grip.

"NO! I served MY TIME! I did EVERYTHING right! I—"

"You hurt a child's protector to access a child," the Clerk said. "That's all the evidence required."

Jonathan was dragged toward the HELL door, still screaming.

The door opened.

He was pulled through.

The door slammed shut.

Silence.

Except for the little girl's quiet sobbing.

Agnes knelt beside her, opened her arms. "It's okay, sweetheart. He's gone. He can't hurt anyone anymore."

The girl threw herself into Agnes's arms, crying into her shoulder.

The dog limped over.

Slowly.

He sat next to them.

The girl pulled back slightly, saw the dog, reached out a trembling hand.

Petted his head.

"Good doggy," she whispered. "You saved me."

The dog's tail wagged. Just once. Gentle.

The digital chime pinged.

Now serving: 847,297-A.

The little girl's number.

She looked up at Agnes. "Is it time?"

"Yes, sweetheart. Your door is opening."

A door—warm light, the smell of sunshine and grass—appeared where she'd been sitting.

The girl stood. Hugged Agnes. "Thank you."

Then she knelt and hugged the dog. "Thank you, good doggy."

She picked up her rabbit and walked through the door.

The door closed.

Silence.

The dog limped back to Marcus and sat down.

Marcus knelt, checked him over. "You okay, buddy?"

The dog licked his hand.

"You're a fucking hero," Marcus said quietly.

Silas was still standing where he'd tackled Jonathan, hands shaking with adrenaline.

The Clerk's voice crackled over the intercom.

"Silas Kane. Return to window."

Everyone froze.

Silas looked up. "What?"

"Return. To. Window."

Silas walked slowly back to the window, dread building in his chest.

The Clerk looked at him. "Revised assessment."

"What? Why?"

"You passed judgment. Earlier. Quote: 'There's a difference. I killed a man in a fight. One man. One moment. This is systematic.' You judged his crime as worse than yours."

"It was worse!"

"That determination is not yours to make."

Silas's blood ran cold. "But I was just—"

"Judging. Yes." The Clerk picked up the stamp. "Your physical intervention to protect the child: Justified. Commendable, even. However. Your earlier statement constituted judgment of another soul. Matthew 7:1."

"I protected a child!"

"And you will not be punished for that. You are being re-sentenced for judging. Not for protecting."

"That's—that's insane!"

THUD.

"Revised destination: Hell."

The room went silent.

Marcus closed his eyes but said nothing.

Father Benjamin looked at the floor.

Sebastian shook his head slowly.

Silas stood there, hollowed out. "But I... I got Heaven. I did my time. I—"

"And then you judged." The Clerk's voice was not unkind. Just... factual. "Return to waiting area."

Silas walked back on legs that felt like they belonged to someone else.

He sat down.

Judge Blackwell, after a long moment, spoke quietly. "Welcome to the club."

Silas looked at him. The man who'd sentenced him fifteen years ago. The man who was also damned for judging.

"Fuck," Silas whispered.

"Yeah," Blackwell said. "Fuck."

The dog limped over to Silas and put his head on his knee.

Silas looked down at him. "I tried to do the right thing, buddy."

The dog's tail wagged.

"Even the dog knows you did right," Marcus said quietly. "But the system doesn't care."

"The system," Silas said, voice hollow, "is fucked."

For the first time, everyone—damned and saved alike—nodded in complete agreement.

Rashid, after a respectful silence, raised his hand slightly. "So... about the virgin allocation—"

"READ THE ROOM!" everyone shouted.

Rashid sat back down, muttering.

The digital chime pinged.

Now serving: 847,299.

Everyone looked around.

Then, slowly, they all looked at the dog.

The dog's ears perked up.

He stood, stretched, limped toward the window.

"The dog has a number," Sebastian said quietly.

They all watched.

The Clerk looked down at the dog.

And smiled.

Episode 8

The Dog

The dog limped to the window.

Everyone watched in absolute silence.

Even Rashid had stopped muttering about virgins.

The dog sat, looking up at the Clerk with patient, trusting eyes. Its tail gave a gentle thump against the linoleum despite the limp.

The Clerk looked down at it.

And smiled.

Not the small, barely-there smile from before.

A real smile. Warm. Almost... fond.

"Hello," the Clerk said softly.

The dog's tail wagged harder.

Marcus leaned forward in his seat. "Is the Clerk... talking to the dog?"

"Looks like it," Sebastian whispered.

The Clerk typed on his keyboard. One-handed. His other hand reached down and scratched behind the dog's ears.

The dog leaned into it, eyes half-closing in bliss.

"Let's see," the Clerk said. "Cause of death: hit by car while protecting owner from same. Owner survived. You did not."

The dog's tail kept wagging.

"Life summary: Rescued from shelter at age two. Loyal companion for eight years. Never bit anyone. Never attacked. Never showed aggression." The Clerk paused. "Until today."

Everyone tensed.

"Subject bit one individual. Jonathan Murphy. Child molester. Assessment: Bite was protective, not aggressive. Justified force."

The dog tilted its head, as if to say, Obviously.

"Additionally," the Clerk continued, scrolling, "subject made contact with all souls in waiting area. Let's review interactions."

He pulled up a screen visible only to him.

"Silas Kane: Subject approached. Silas petted subject. Showed kindness. Passed."

Silas sat up straighter.

"Marcus Lambert: Subject approached. Marcus petted subject. Showed kindness. Passed."

Marcus's eyes widened.

"Sebastian Caine: Subject approached. Sebastian petted subject despite claiming unworthiness. Showed vulnerability. Passed."

Sebastian made a small, choked sound.

"Judge Arthur Blackwell: Subject approached. Judge ignored subject. Showed indifference. Failed."

Blackwell's face went pale.

"Father Benjamin Haas: Subject approached. Father refused contact. Showed... self-condemnation manifesting as rejection of grace. Failed."

Father Benjamin's hands started shaking.

"Agnes Whitmore: Subject approached. Agnes rejected subject as 'unclean.' Failed. Later: Agnes returned, showed kindness after molester incident. Partial redemption noted but insufficient to overturn initial failure."

Agnes started crying quietly.

"Jonathan Murphy: Subject approached. Murphy kicked subject. Showed violence toward innocent. Failed catastrophically."

No one had anything to say about that.

"Rashid Al-Mansour: Subject did not approach. Rashid showed no interest in subject. Mutual indifference. Inconclusive."

Rashid shifted uncomfortably.

The Clerk looked down at the dog. "Do you know what your name is?"

The dog's tail wagged.

The Clerk typed something. Turned the screen around.

On it, in simple letters: TEST

The room went silent.

Then—

"Oh my God," Marcus breathed.

"His name is Test," Sebastian said slowly. "His name is Test."

"We were being tested," Silas said. "The whole time. By the dog."

Father Benjamin made a sound like he'd been punched. "I refused to pet him. I refused because I thought I was unworthy."

"And I rejected him as unclean," Agnes whispered. "Just like I rejected everyone else."

Blackwell just stared at his hands. "I ignored him. I didn't even... I was too busy being angry to notice a dog."

"The simplest test," Marcus said, staring at Test. "Just... be kind to a dog. That's it. That's all we had to do."

"And most of you failed," the Clerk said. Not unkindly. Just... factually.

He looked at Test. "Good boy. Very good boy. You performed your function perfectly."

Test's tail wagged so hard his whole backend wiggled.

"Destination," the Clerk said, and picked up the stamp.

Everyone held their breath.

THUD.

"Heaven. Immediate processing. No waiting."

A door opened. Not the INTAKE door. Not the regular door.

A different door.

Warm light spilled out. It smelled like grass after rain, and sunshine, and every good thing anyone had ever felt.

It smelled like home.

Test stood up, tail wagging.

He turned back to look at the waiting room.

At all of them.

Then he limped through the door.

The door closed.

Silence.

Then Sebastian started laughing. Broken, slightly hysterical. "We got tested by a dog. A dog named Test. And most of us failed."

"The dog got immediate processing," Marcus said, dazed. "No waiting. Straight to Heaven."

"Because he was the only one who passed his own test," Father Benjamin said hollowly. "He protected. He showed kindness. He judged no one. He just... loved."

"And we failed him," Agnes said, tears streaming down her face.

"Not all of us," Silas said quietly. "Some of us passed."

"And you still ended up in Hell," Blackwell said. "Because you judged the molester."

"Yeah." Silas laughed once, bitter. "I passed Test. But I failed the system."

"Maybe," Marcus said slowly, "that's the point. Maybe Test was checking if we had basic decency. And the system is checking if we think we're better than others."

"So even being decent isn't enough," Sebastian said. "You have to be decent without thinking you're better than the indecent."

"That's impossible," Blackwell said.

"Maybe," Father Benjamin said. "Or maybe that's what grace is. Being kind without keeping score."

They sat with that for a long moment.

Then Rashid raised his hand. "So... the dog got immediate processing. Can I file a motion for expedited—"

"NO!" everyone shouted.

"I was just asking," Rashid muttered, sitting back down.

Agnes stood up. Walked to where Test had been sitting. Knelt down.

Touched the spot on the floor.

"I'm sorry," she whispered. "I'm so sorry."

Father Benjamin joined her. Knelt beside her.

"Me too," he said.

Marcus looked at Silas. "You passed Test."

"Lot of good it did me," Silas said.

"Still counts for something."

"Does it?"

Marcus thought about it. "Yeah. I think it does. You protected an innocent creature. The system damned you for judging the molester, but... you passed the important test. The simple one. Be kind to a dog." He smiled slightly. "In my book, that counts."

"Your book doesn't determine eternal destinations," Blackwell said.

"Neither did yours," Marcus shot back. "That was the whole problem."

Blackwell had no response.

Sebastian stood up, walked to the window. Looked at the Clerk.

"Can I ask you something?"

"Briefly."

"Was Test always going to Heaven?"

"Yes."

"So he didn't need to be tested."

"Correct. He was not being tested. He was the test."

"And he knew it? The whole time?"

The Clerk's expression softened. "Test knew exactly what he was. He knew his purpose. And he fulfilled it perfectly. Every tail wag. Every gentle approach. Every moment of offered grace. He knew."

"He knew most of us would fail," Sebastian said.

"Yes."

"And he offered grace anyway."

"Yes."

Sebastian nodded slowly. "That's... that's actually beautiful."

"It is," the Clerk agreed.

Sebastian returned to his seat.

They all sat there, in the waiting room, feeling the absence of a scruffy brown-and-white dog.

The dog who had been the only perfect soul among them.

"I'm going to miss that dog," Marcus said.

"Me too," Silas said.

"Me too," Agnes whispered.

Even Blackwell, after a long moment, nodded.

The digital chime pinged.

NOW SERVING: 847,300.

Everyone looked around.

"Who's left?" Marcus asked.

They did a count.

Then they heard a toilet flush.

From the bathroom no one had paid attention to, a man emerged.

Expensive suit. Rolex. The kind of smile that came from a lifetime of getting exactly what he wanted.

He looked at them all staring at him.

"What?" he said. "Did I miss something?"

Episode 9

The Billionaire

The man who emerged from the bathroom looked like he'd stepped out of a Forbes cover shoot.

Expensive suit. Rolex that cost more than most people's cars. Hair that had been professionally styled that morning—or whatever passed for morning in the afterlife. The kind of confident smile that came from a lifetime of getting exactly what he wanted.

He looked around the waiting room, taking in the exhausted, broken faces staring back at him.

"What?" he said. "Did I miss something?"

Everyone just stared.

Marcus broke the silence. "How long have you been in there?"

"I don't know. Twenty minutes? There's no clock." The man straightened his tie. "Needed a moment to collect myself. Death is rather... disorienting."

"Twenty minutes," Sebastian repeated. "You missed everything."

"Well, I'm here now." The man walked to an empty seat, sat down like he owned the place. "So. This is the afterlife. Bit more bureaucratic than advertised, isn't it?"

Rashid muttered something in Arabic.

Agnes clutched her rosary tighter.

The Billionaire looked around. "Is there coffee? Please tell me there's coffee."

"No coffee," Silas said flatly.

"Pity." The Billionaire crossed his legs. "So what's the process here? Take a number, wait your turn, get sorted?"

"Something like that," Marcus said.

"Efficient. I appreciate efficiency." The Billionaire pulled out his ticket. Looked at it. "847,300. Excellent. Shouldn't be long now."

Judge Blackwell leaned toward Silas, voice low. "I already hate him."

"Yeah," Silas said. "Me too."

They sat in silence for a moment. The damned and the saved and the perpetually pending (Rashid), all waiting for the next number to be called.

Then Silas laughed. Quiet, bitter.

Blackwell looked at him. "What?"

"Nothing. Just... thinking about something."

"Care to share?"

Silas looked at the Judge. Really looked at him. The man who'd sentenced him to fifteen years. The man who was now sentenced to eternity in Hell. Both of them, together, damned for the same sin.

"You know what's funny?" Silas said.

"I doubt anything about this is funny."

"When I was in Pelican Bay. Year eight, maybe nine. I was lying in my cell, and I started thinking about... this. The afterlife. Judgment. All of it."

Blackwell raised an eyebrow. "You found religion in prison?"

"No. Nothing like that. I just... I'd confessed, right? Turned myself in. Pled guilty. Did my time. And I t hought... if there really is a system, if confession plus punishment equals redemption, then mathematically..." He laughed again. "Mathematically, I should be fine."

Blackwell stared at him. "You calculated your way into Heaven?"

"I didn't think it would actually work. It was just... a thought experiment. A way to pass the time. But I figured, if the rules are the rules, then..." He shrugged. "Here we are."

"You gamed the system."

"I followed the system. There's a difference."

"Is there?"

Silas thought about that. "I don't know. Maybe not. Maybe that's why I'm in Hell now. Maybe thinking you can game divine justice is itself—" He gestured vaguely. "—judging divine justice. Assuming you know how it works."

Blackwell was quiet for a long moment. Then: "And meeting me here?"

"Gold," Silas said, smiling despite everything. "Pure gold. The man who sentenced me, damned for the same reason I am. Both of us judged. Both of us thought we knew better than the system."

"I was upholding the law."

"And I was following it. And we both ended up in Hell."

Blackwell laughed. It was a broken, exhausted sound. "This is absurd."

"Yeah."

"We're both going to the same place. Forever."

"Looks like it."

"I sentenced you to fifteen years. And now we get eternity together."

"Ironic, right?"

Blackwell shook his head. "I don't know if that's irony or just cosmic cruelty."

"Maybe both."

They sat with that for a moment.

Then Blackwell said, quietly: "For what it's worth... I'm sorry. For the sentencing. For—" He gestured help-lessly. "For all of it."

Silas looked at him, surprised. "You're apologizing?"

"Seems like the right time. We're both damned any-way."

"Yeah." Silas nodded slowly. "Yeah, we are." He paused. "For what it's worth... I'm sorry too. For judging you. For thinking I was better because I'd 'served my time' and you were just a—"

"A judgmental asshole?"

"Yeah. That."

They looked at each other. Two men. A murderer and a judge. Both damned for thinking they knew better.

"Hell's going to be interesting," Blackwell said.

"At least we'll have company," Silas replied.

The digital chime pinged.

Now serving: 847,300.

The Billionaire stood up, smoothed his suit. "That's me. Wish me luck, gentlemen."

He walked to the window with the confidence of a man who'd never been told 'no' in his entire life.

The Clerk looked up. "Name."

"Harrison Caldwell III."

"Occupation: Venture capitalist, CEO of Caldwell Holdings. Net worth at time of death: 8.4 billion dollars."

Harrison smiled. "Eight point six, actually. The markets were up."

The Clerk didn't react. "Cause of death: Heart attack. Age 52. Massive cardiac event during charity gala."

"Ironic, isn't it? Died while raising money for children's hospitals." Harrison leaned on the counter like he was closing a deal. "I assume that counts in my favor?"

The Clerk scrolled. "Charitable giving: 847 million dollars over lifetime. Hospitals, schools, disaster relief, cancer research."

"See? I was a good man. Generous. I built an empire and I gave back."

"Yes. Let's examine that giving." The Clerk's fingers moved across the keyboard. "St. Mary's Hospital: 50

million dollar donation. Tax deduction: 50 million dollars. Net cost to donor: zero."

Harrison's smile faltered slightly. "That's... how charitable giving works. The tax code encourages—"

"Caldwell Children's Wing: 100 million dollar donation. Naming rights secured. PR value: estimated 340 million in positive brand exposure. Tax deduction: 100 million. Net cost: zero. Net gain: 240 million in brand value."

"I still gave the money!"

"You invested the money," the Clerk corrected. "Every donation came with benefits. Tax breaks. Naming rights. Positive press. Board seats. Political access. You gave 847 million and received, in tangible and intangible benefits, approximately 1.2 billion in return."

Harrison's face was reddening. "That's not—I helped people! Children got medical care! Students got scholarships!"

"Yes. They did. And you profited from their suffering." The Clerk looked up. "Matthew 6:2. 'When you give to the needy, do not announce it with trumpets, as the hypocrites do in the synagogues and on the streets, to be honored by others. Truly I tell you, they have received their reward in full.'"

"I received nothing!"

"You received everything. Fame. Fortune. Tax breaks. Social capital. Every dollar you gave came back to you multiplied. You turned charity into profit."

"But people were helped!"

"Yes. As a side effect of your self-interest." The Clerk picked up the stamp. "The question is not whether good was done. The question is: Why did you do it?"

Harrison was sweating now. "Because... because it was the right thing to do!"

"Was it? Or was it because Forbes was watching? Because your shareholders expected it? Because the tax code rewarded it?"

Silence.

"Mr. Caldwell. If there had been no tax breaks, no naming rights, no publicity—would you still have given?"

Harrison opened his mouth. Closed it.

"That's what I thought." The Clerk raised the stamp.

"Wait! I—I built a company! I employed 50,000 people! I created value! I—"

"You paid minimum wage whenever legally possible. You fought unionization efforts. You moved production overseas to exploit cheaper labor. You laid off 3,000 workers the same year you bought your fourth vacation home."

"That's just business!"

"Yes. It is. And business," the Clerk said, "is not righteousness."

THUD.

"Destination: Hell."

Harrison staggered backward. "No. No, this is—I gave billions!"

"You invested billions. In yourself. Next."

"I demand to speak to a supervisor! I want to appeal! This is—"

"Form 7734. Processing time: eternity. Return to waiting area."

"This is BULLSHIT!" Harrison was shouting now. "I built an empire! I helped thousands of people! I—"

"You helped yourself and thousands benefited accidentally. There's a difference." The Clerk's voice was flat. "Next."

Harrison stood there, breathing hard, face red.

Then he turned and walked back to the waiting room.

Sat down heavily.

Everyone watched him.

"Well," Sebastian said after a moment. "That went well."

Harrison looked around at them. "This is insane. I gave money. Real money. Not thoughts and prayers. Not empty gestures. Actual, tangible help."

"With strings attached," Marcus said quietly.

"So what?! People were still helped!"

"But that's not why you did it," Father Benjamin said, voice hollow. "You did it for the tax breaks. For the recognition. For yourself."

"And that makes me evil?!"

"No," Agnes said. "It makes you... not good. There's a difference."

Harrison laughed, bitter. "This coming from someone going to Hell herself?"

"Yes," Agnes said simply. "It is."

Harrison slumped in his chair, deflated.

Rashid, who'd been quiet this entire time, raised his hand.

"Don't," everyone said in unison.

"I was just going to ask—"

"NO."

Rashid sat back down.

The room fell into exhausted silence.

Silas looked at Judge Blackwell. "You know what the really funny part is?"

"What?"

"The only person in this room who's actually getting Heaven is Marcus. The atheist. The guy who never believed in any of this. Never tried to earn it. Never calculated the odds. Just... helped people because he thought it was the right thing to do."

Marcus looked uncomfortable. "I mean..."

"No, he's right," Sebastian said. "You're the only one who's actually getting out clean. The rest of us? We're all fucked in one way or another."

"I'm going to Heaven," Harrison protested.

"You're going to Heaven as punishment," Sebastian corrected. "Trust me, it's not the same thing."

"And I'm stuck in virgin allocation purgatory," Rashid muttered.

"You are going to Hell, with us" Blackwell said, gesturing to himself, Agnes, Father Benjamin, Silas, and Harrison.

"The dog went to Heaven," Agnes said softly. "He was good. Pure. He didn't judge. He just... loved."

Everyone nodded at that.

"I miss that dog," Marcus said.

"Me too," several people echoed.

The digital chime pinged.

Now serving: 847,301.

Everyone looked around.

"Is there anyone else?" Sebastian asked.

They counted. Judge, Agnes, Father Benjamin, Silas, Marcus, Sebastian, Rashid, Harrison...

"Wait," Marcus said. "Where's—"

The bathroom door opened.

A young man stepped out. Maybe twenty-five. Wearing a hoodie. He looked confused, lost, terrified.

"Sorry," he said quietly. "I've been in there for... I don't know how long. I heard screaming. Is everything okay?"

Everyone just stared at him.

"Oh God," Silas said. "There's another one?"

The young man walked nervously to the window.

The Clerk looked up.

"Name."

"Um. David Lambert. David Lambert."

Silas sat up straight and turned to Marcus. "Lambert? Are you—"

"Related to him?" The Clerk looked at Marcus. "Yes. Younger brother. David Lambert."

Marcus went pale.

David looked back, saw Marcus, and his face crumpled. "Oh God. Marcus? You're—you're here too?"

"David," Marcus breathed. "What happened? How did you—"

The Clerk interrupted. "Cause of death: Drug overdose. Fentanyl-laced heroin. Age 25."

Marcus stood up. "No. No, he was clean. He'd been clean for—"

"Fourteen months," the Clerk confirmed. "Relapse occurred three weeks ago. Fatal overdose occurred sixteen minutes ago."

David was crying now. "I'm sorry, Marcus. I'm so sorry. I tried. I really tried."

"This is Hell," Marcus said, and his voice broke. "This is actually Hell. Watching my brother—"

"Sir, please sit down," the Clerk said.

Marcus sat, but he couldn't look away from David.

The Clerk looked at David. "Shall we begin?"

David nodded, wiping his eyes.

"Life summary: Struggled with addiction from age seventeen. Multiple rehabilitation attempts. Stole from family to fund habit. Hurt people who loved you. Relapsed repeatedly."

David nodded, voice small. "I know."

"However. You tried. Fourteen months of sobriety. Attended meetings. Helped other addicts. Worked to rebuild relationships. Relapsed not from lack of trying, but from—" The Clerk paused. "From pain you couldn't bear."

David was sobbing now.

"The question before the system: Is addiction a choice or a disease? Is relapse a moral failing or a symptom?"

No one in the room dared breathe.

The Clerk picked up the stamp.

"David Lambert. You hurt people. You stole. You lied. You relapsed. You died alone in an apartment, and no one will find you for four days."

David's shoulders shook with sobs.

"However. You fought. Every day, you fought. And on your last day, your final conscious thought was—" The Clerk read from the screen. "—'I'm sorry, Marcus. I'm so sorry.'"

THUD.

"Destination: Heaven."

The room erupted.

"WHAT?!" Harrison was on his feet. "I gave BIL-LIONS and he gets HEAVEN?!"

Marcus was crying, hands over his face.

David just stood there, stunned. "But I... I failed. I relapsed. I—"

"You tried," the Clerk said simply. "That's more than most. Return to waiting area. Your door will open when processing is complete."

David walked back on shaking legs.

Marcus stood, crossed the room, and pulled his brother into a hug.

They stood there, both crying, while everyone watched.

"I'm so sorry," David whispered. "I tried so hard."

"I know," Marcus said. "I know you did."

Harrison was pacing, furious. "This is insane! A drug addict gets Heaven?!"

"He tried to be better," Father Benjamin said quietly. "That's all that mattered. He tried."

"I tried!" Harrison shouted. "I gave money! I built things! I—"

"You succeeded," Agnes said. "That's the difference. He tried and failed and kept trying. You succeeded and took credit. Which one is more worthy of grace?"

Harrison had no answer.

Silas looked at Judge Blackwell. "You know what? Maybe Hell won't be so bad."

"How do you figure?"

"At least we won't have to listen to him." Silas gestured at Harrison.

"Oh, I'm definitely going to be there," Harrison muttered. "Apparently trying hard counts more than actual results."

"Yeah," Marcus said, still holding his brother. "It does."

The digital chime pinged.

Now serving: 847,305.

Everyone looked around.

Everyone had been called.

Except...

Rashid stood up. "Finally! That's—that's my number, right? The virgin allocation must be—"

"No," the Clerk's voice crackled over the intercom. "That number does not exist. Please sit down."

Rashid froze. "What?"

"There is no 847,305. Processing is complete."

"But my virgins! The allocation! You said—"

"I said you were pending. You remain pending. Sit down."

Rashid sat slowly, face pale.

"So... I just... wait?"

"Yes."

"For how long?"

"Eternity."

Rashid looked around the room. At all the people who'd been judged, sentenced, processed.

At the empty chairs.

At the doors that would soon open.

"This is my Hell," he whispered. "Isn't it? Waiting forever for something that's never coming."

The Clerk didn't respond.

Rashid sat down.

Started crying.

"The waiting room," the Clerk's voice announced. "Will now process final door assignments. Please stand when your destination is called."

Everyone stood.

Long pause.

Nothing happened.

The doors remained closed.

Judge Blackwell looked around. "Uh... now what?"

Silence.

Then, from the intercom:

"System error. Door malfunction. Please remain standing. Estimated wait time: calculating..."

A long, mechanical pause.

"Estimated wait time: unknown."

Everyone looked at each other.

"You have GOT to be kidding me," Sebastian said.

Episode 10

The Doors

The grinding sound grew louder.

The floor vibrated.

Everyone stood frozen, staring at the doors as they slowly—painfully—began to open.

The Heaven door went first.

Warm light spilled out. The smell of cut grass and sunshine and something else—something that made Marcus's chest ache with a feeling he couldn't name. Home, maybe. Or peace. Or the absence of every bad thing that had ever happened.

The Hell door opened next.

No fire. No screaming. No demons with pitchforks.

Just... darkness. Not scary darkness. Just the absence of light. Like a hallway with the lights off.

Everyone stared.

"Well," Sebastian said. "That's anticlimactic."

The Clerk's voice crackled over the intercom. "Final boarding. Heaven: Marcus Lambert. David Lambert. Sebastian Caine."

Marcus looked at his brother. David was crying again, but smiling through it.

"We made it," David whispered.

"Yeah," Marcus said. "We did."

Sebastian stood slowly. Looked at the Heaven door. At the light. At the warmth.

"I don't want to go," he said quietly.

"You have to," the Clerk said.

"I know." Sebastian laughed once, broken. "That's the whole problem, isn't it?"

Marcus walked over, put a hand on Sebastian's shoulder. "Hey. Maybe it won't be as bad as you think."

"It'll be worse," Sebastian said. "But thanks for trying."

The three of them walked to the Heaven door.

Marcus turned back once. Looked at Silas. The murderer who'd protected a child. The man who'd been kind to a dog.

"Good luck," Marcus said.

Silas nodded. "You too."

Marcus, David, and Sebastian stepped through the door.

***

Marcus blinked.

He was standing in a field. Endless grass. Blue sky. The kind of perfect day that didn't exist in real life because real life always had traffic or deadlines or something to worry about.

David was next to him, laughing, spinning around with his arms out.

"Marcus, look! It's—it's beautiful!"

And then Marcus saw her.

His mother.

Standing at the edge of the field, smiling, arms open.

David saw her too. Made a sound between a laugh and a sob, and ran.

Marcus followed.

They reached her together and she pulled them both into a hug and it smelled like her perfume and her cooking and every good memory Marcus had ever had, and he realized he was crying and he didn't care.

"My boys," she said. "My beautiful boys."

"Mom," David sobbed. "I'm sorry. I'm so sorry I—"

"Shh. You're here now. That's all that matters."

They stood there, the three of them, in the perfect field under the perfect sky.

Marcus looked around. "Is this... is this it? Forever?"

His mother smiled. "This is the beginning."

And somewhere, far away, Marcus heard music. Laughter. Voices.

It was perfect.

***

Sebastian stepped through the door and immediately wanted to scream.

Soft grass under his feet. Gentle breeze. Warm sunshine that felt like a hug he didn't ask for.

A woman appeared. She looked kind. Motherly. She smiled at him.

"Welcome," she said. "You must be tired. Come. Rest."

"I don't want to rest," Sebastian said.

"I know. Come anyway."

She led him to a bench. Soft cushions. A view of a lake so calm it looked like glass.

"Sit."

Sebastian sat.

It was comfortable.

Perfectly, unbearably comfortable.

"No," he whispered.

"Yes," she said gently. "This is your eternity. Peace. Comfort. Kindness. Forever."

Sebastian started laughing. Then crying. Then both.

The woman sat next to him and put a hand on his shoulder.

It was the gentlest touch he'd ever felt.

It was torture.

"Welcome to Heaven," she said softly.

Sebastian covered his face with his hands and wept.

***

The Heaven door closed.

The Clerk's voice: "Hell: Judge Arthur Blackwell. Agnes Whitmore. Father Benjamin Haas. Silas Kane. Harrison Caldwell III."

They stood.

Agnes clutched her rosary one last time.

Father Benjamin closed his eyes, whispering something that might have been a prayer.

Harrison was still muttering about tax deductions and ROI.

Judge Blackwell looked at Silas. "Ready?"

"No," Silas said. "You?"

"Not even a little."

"Good. Let's go."

They walked to the Hell door.

Stood at the threshold.

The darkness beyond wasn't hot. Wasn't cold. Just... empty.

"Well," Agnes said quietly. "I suppose we earned this."

"Yeah," Father Benjamin said. "We did."

Harrison pushed forward. "Let's just get this over with."

They stepped through.

***

The door closed behind them.

They stood in darkness for a moment.

Then lights flickered on.

Fluorescent. Buzzing. That same sickly white light.

They were in a waiting room.

Another waiting room.

Plastic chairs. Beige walls. Linoleum floors. A "TAKE A NUMBER" machine in the corner.

A window with a Clerk behind it.

The Clerk looked up. Not the same Clerk. But the same expression. Bored. Exhausted. Done with eternity.

"Welcome to Hell," the Clerk said. "Please take a number."

They stared.

"You have got to be kidding me," Harrison said.

"I assure you, we are not." The Clerk gestured to the machine. "Take a number. Have a seat. We'll process you shortly."

"Process us for what?" Agnes demanded.

"Your eternal assignment. Hell has multiple departments. We need to determine which one is appropriate for your specific sins."

"How long will that take?" Father Benjamin asked.

"Eternity has no timeline."

Judge Blackwell walked to the machine. Pulled a ticket.

000,001

He looked at it. Started laughing.

"What?" Silas asked.

Blackwell showed him the ticket. "We're first in line."

Silas looked at the number. At the waiting room. At the Clerk behind the window.

And he started laughing too.

"What's funny?" Agnes asked.

"This," Silas said, gesturing around. "This is Hell. Not fire. Not torture. Just... this. Forever."

Agnes looked around. At the plastic chairs. The fluorescent lights. The endless, bureaucratic eternity stretching before them.

She sat down heavily.

"Oh," she whispered. "Oh no."

Harrison was pacing. "This is unacceptable. I demand to speak to—"

"Form 7734," the Clerk said without looking up. "Fill it out. Return it to the window. Processing time: eternity."

Harrison stopped pacing. Sat down. Put his head in his hands.

Father Benjamin sat next to Agnes. "I'm sorry," he said quietly. "For everything. For failing you. For failing... everyone."

"I know," Agnes said. "Me too."

They sat in silence.

The digital chime pinged.

Now serving: 000,001.

Judge Blackwell stood. Looked at his ticket. Looked at Silas.

"Wish me luck."

"You're in Hell," Silas said. "There is no luck."

"Fair point."

Blackwell walked to the window.

Silas watched him go, then sat down in one of the plastic chairs.

They were just as uncomfortable as the ones in the first waiting room.

He laughed once. Quiet. Bitter.

Harrison looked at him. "What's so funny?"

"Nothing," Silas said. "Absolutely nothing."

"Then why are you laughing?"

"Because," Silas said, "if I don't laugh, I'll scream. And I have eternity to do that. Might as well pace myself."

Harrison stared at him. Then, despite everything, laughed too.

It was a broken laugh.

But it was something.

Judge Blackwell returned from the window. Sat down next to Silas.

"Well?" Silas asked.

"They're reviewing my file. Could take anywhere from a few minutes to a few millennia."

"Of course."

They sat in silence.

Then Blackwell spoke, voice quiet. "This is your fault, you know."

Silas looked at him. At the man who'd sentenced him fifteen years ago. At the man sitting next to him in Hell's waiting room.

"Still?" Silas asked.

Blackwell nodded slowly. "Forever."

Silas thought about that. About Ray-Ray. About the tire iron. About fifteen years in Pelican Bay. About 847 letters. About getting Heaven and losing it. About protecting a child and being damned anyway.

About sitting here, in Hell, next to the judge who'd sent him to prison.

For eternity.

He started laughing again.

"What?" Blackwell asked.

"Nothing," Silas said. "Just... the universe has a fucked-up sense of humor."

"Yeah," Blackwell said. "It does."

They sat there.

Together.

Forever.

The digital chime pinged.

Now serving: 000,002.

Agnes stood. Walked to the window.

The waiting continued.

As it always would.

THE END

Oh, wait...

***

The original waiting room.

Empty now.

Silent.

The fluorescent lights still buzzed.

The plastic chairs sat in neat rows, unoccupied.

Except for one.

Rashid sat alone, hands folded in his lap, staring at nothing.

He'd been sitting there for... how long? Hours? Days? Time didn't work right here.

Everyone else was gone.

Processed. Assigned. Moved on to their eternities.

But not him.

He stood slowly. Walked to the window.

The Clerk was still there. Always there.

"Excuse me," Rashid said quietly.

The Clerk looked up.

"I need to understand. The virgin allocation. The processing. How much longer?"

The Clerk typed on his keyboard. Scrolled.

"Still pending."

"But everyone else is gone. I'm the only one left."

"Correct."

"So surely—surely now that the queue is clear, my case can be—"

"Pending."

Rashid's voice broke. "The virgins. Are they coming? Will they ever come?"

The Clerk looked at him for a long moment.

"Pending."

"That's not an answer."

"It's the only answer you're going to get."

Rashid stood there, trembling.

"This is Hell," he whispered. "Isn't it? This is my Hell. Waiting forever for something that's never coming."

"Take another number," the Clerk said.

Rashid walked to the "TAKE A NUMBER" machine.

Pulled a ticket.

Looked at it.

∞

Infinity.

He stared at the symbol.

Looked around the empty waiting room.

At the chairs no one would ever sit in again.

At the doors that would never open for him.

He walked back to his seat.

Sat down.

Alone.

The Clerk returned to his paperwork.

The fluorescent lights buzzed.

Time—or whatever passed for time here—stretched out before him.

Forever.

Rashid closed his eyes.

Opened them.

The waiting room was still there.

Still empty.

Still eternal.

He would wait.

He had no choice.

The virgins weren't coming.
They had never been coming.
But he would wait anyway.
Forever.

THE END OF PART ONE

13

YES, THIRTEEN

U Fiction Publishing LLC

Episode 11

The Bystander

Daniel Park had been in the room for the entire performance.

He sat in the far back corner, near the water cooler that didn't work. He hadn't spoken when the Judge raged. He hadn't whispered when the Murderer was forgiven. He hadn't moved when the Saint was damned.

He was good at that. Being furniture.

When the chaos erupted—when Jonathan Murphy walked toward the little girl—Daniel had been the closest one to them.

He saw the look in Jonathan's eyes before anyone else. He saw the dog's hackles rise. He heard Marcus scream, "Someone grab him!"

Daniel had looked up. He made eye contact with Jonathan. He saw the intent.

And he froze.

He calculated the distance. He calculated the risk. *He's big. He looks unstable. If I intervene, I might get hurt. It's not my business. Someone else will handle it.*

So he watched.

He watched the dog lunge. watched the kick. Watched Silas—a convicted murderer—do what Daniel wouldn't.

Now, the room was empty.

The Heaven door had closed behind Marcus, David, and Sebastian. The Hell door had swallowed the Judge, the Priest, and the others. The dog—Test—was gone.

It was just Daniel. And the Clerk.

The digital chime didn't ping. The Clerk just looked over the rim of his glasses.

"You can stop hiding now, Mr. Park."

Daniel stood up. His legs felt heavy, like they were filled with lead. He walked to the window.

"I wasn't hiding," Daniel said. "I was just... waiting my turn."

"You were blending in," the Clerk corrected. "It's your signature move."

The Clerk tapped the keyboard. "Daniel Park. Age 47. Cause of death: Aneurysm. Happened while you were filming a fight in a grocery store parking lot instead of calling 911."

Daniel flinched. "I was documenting evidence."

"You were hungry for likes. Let's review the record."

The Clerk didn't scroll. He just stared at Daniel.

"Philadelphia, 2008. Domestic dispute next door. You heard the screaming. You turned up the volume on your TV."

"I didn't know the full context," Daniel stammered. "Calling the police could have escalated it."

"The context," the Clerk said dryly, "was a broken orbital bone. But you got to finish your show."

"I—"

"Chicago, 2015. A teenager being harassed on the subway. You moved to the next car."

"There were bigger guys there! Why didn't *they* do anything?"

"We judged them yesterday," the Clerk said. "We're talking about you."

Daniel gripped the counter. "I never hurt anyone. I followed the law. I paid my taxes. I was a nice guy."

"You were a camera," the Clerk said. "A recording device with a pulse."

"That's not a sin!"

"Isn't it?" The Clerk pointed a long finger at the spot on the floor where Jonathan had stood. "Ten minutes ago. A child was threatened. You were three feet away. Marcus yelled for help. You looked at your shoes."

"I... I froze."

"Silas didn't. And Silas is a murderer." The Clerk leaned forward. "That's the uncomfortable math, isn't it? The man who bashed a skull in with a tire iron had more moral courage in his pinky finger than you displayed in forty-seven years."

"I was scared!" Daniel shouted. "I'm not a hero! I'm just a normal person! Self-preservation is a basic instinct!"

"And apathy is a choice."

The Clerk picked up a stamp.

It wasn't red. It wasn't blue. It was clear. Made of glass. Transparent.

"So," Daniel breathed, trying to steady his heart. "Where do I go? The Vestibule? Limbo? Somewhere... neutral?"

"Neutrality is a myth, Mr. Park. You chose your side every time you refused to take one."

The Clerk raised the glass stamp.

"You spent your life pretending you were powerless," the Clerk said. His voice wasn't angry. It was terrifyingly matter-of-fact. "You told yourself you *couldn't* make a difference, so you didn't have to try."

"Yes," Daniel whispered. "I was powerless."

"Now," the Clerk said, bringing the stamp down. "You actually are."

THUD.

"Destination: Witness."

Daniel blinked. "What?"

"You like to watch? You like to be the bystander? Then be the ultimate bystander."

The floor beneath Daniel didn't open. It simply... dissolved.

"Wait!" Daniel scrambled, grabbing for the counter. His hands passed through the laminate like it was smoke. "What's happening?!"

"You're going back," the Clerk said, turning back to his paperwork. "Have fun."

Daniel fell.

He fell through the gray linoleum, through the darkness, through the fabric of the world.

He landed hard.

Concrete. Wet pavement. The smell of rain and exhaust.

He scrambled up. He knew this street. It was outside his old apartment in Seattle.

A scream cut through the air.

Daniel turned.

In the alleyway, a man had a woman pinned against the bricks. He had a hand over her mouth. Her eyes were wide, white with terror.

Instinct kicked in. The instinct Daniel had suppressed for forty-seven years.

"HEY!" Daniel roared. "GET OFF HER!"

He charged. He balled his fist. He swung with everything he had at the attacker's head.

His fist passed through the man's skull like mist.

There was no impact. No sound.

The attacker didn't even blink. He didn't know Daniel was there.

The woman looked right through Daniel. She was staring at the empty air where he stood, screaming for help.

"I'm here!" Daniel screamed. He grabbed the attacker's arm. His fingers sank through the flesh, cold and useless. "I'M HERE! STOP IT!"

The attacker ripped the woman's purse from her shoulder. He struck her across the face.

Daniel threw himself between them. A human shield.

The blow passed right through Daniel's chest and connected with the woman.

She fell.

Daniel stood over her, screaming, waving his arms, trying to touch her, trying to comfort her, trying to be *solid*.

"Please!" he sobbed. "Please, I'm trying to help! Can't you see me?!"

She couldn't.

The attacker ran off. The woman lay on the wet pavement, weeping.

Daniel knelt beside her. He tried to brush the hair from her face. His hand was smoke.

He realized then.

He looked up at the sky. At the millions of windows in the city. At the millions of alleys.

"You will witness every injustice," the Clerk's voice echoed in his mind. "You will be present for every moment of suffering. You will be desperate to intervene. And you will be unable to do anything except watch."

"No," Daniel whispered. "No, please."

"Forever."

A siren wailed in the distance.

Daniel stood up. He felt a pull. A tug in his chest.

Someone else was screaming. Blocks away.

He didn't want to go.

But he was a witness. And the show never ends.

Daniel Park faded into the mist, pulled toward the next tragedy he could do absolutely nothing about.

Episode 12

The Influencer

Jessica White had been dead for approximately nine minutes when she realized nobody was filming it.

No phone. No camera. No ring light. Just her and a waiting room that looked like every DMV had fucked a funeral home and this was their ugly baby.

She'd taken her number—□□□,□□□—and sat down, already mentally drafting the post.

"POV: You die and the afterlife has ZERO aesthetic [skull emote, obviously] Someone fire God's interior designer challenge #AfterlifeFail #JusticeForTheDeceased"

Except there was no phone. No laptop. No anything.

Just fluorescent lights that made everyone look like they'd been embalmed twice, chairs designed by someone who hated the human spine, and a smell that was probably industrial cleaner but felt like bureaucratic resignation in aerosol form.

The first real sign she might be in Hell.

Around her, chaos. A judge muttering about injustice. A woman speed-reading rosary beads.

People were being called to a window. Getting verdicts. Coming back looking either vindicated or destroyed.

Jessica watched, already planning the thread.

Then remembered: no thread. No followers. No engagement metrics.

Just her.

Uncomfortable silence.

The digital chime pinged.

Now serving: 847,303

Jessica stood, smoothing her dress. Force of habit. Always camera-ready, even when there was no camera.

She walked to the window. The Clerk looked up with the expression of someone who'd processed a million souls and found all of them exhausting.

"Jessica White."

"Hi! Yes! That's me!" She smiled. Bright. Engaging. Authentic™.

The Clerk didn't smile back.

His fingers clicked across the keyboard. "Lifestyle influencer. Dead at thirty-one. Car accident. 2.4 million followers."

Jessica felt a little flutter. Even dead, the numbers still—

"Not here," the Clerk added. "Here you have zero."

The flutter died.

"Oh. Well. I mean, technically—"

"Verified on Instagram, TikTok, and Twitter."

"It's X now," Jessica corrected.

"Whatever." The Clerk didn't look up. "It'll change names again. You won't be there to witness it."

Silence.

"So," Jessica tried again. "About my—"

"July 2019. Mental health awareness post. 'It's okay to not be okay <3 #EndTheStigma.' Posted the same day a celebrity died. 47,000 likes. Three affiliate links."

"I was raising awareness!"

"You were raising your click-through rate."

"People needed resources!"

"You needed commission." The Clerk scrolled. "You made $3,200 that week. From grief. Well done."

Jessica's smile was cracking. "I was helping—"

"September 2020. Black square. 'Black Lives Matter' in bio for six days. No donations. No protest attendance. No follow-up posts. But you did make sure everyone saw that you posted it."

"I was showing solidarity!"

"You were showing up in the algorithm."

"That's not—"

"March 2021. International Women's Day. Posted about empowerment. Got 4,847 comments from women asking for advice. You responded to twelve. All from verified accounts. The woman asking how to leave her abusive relationship? Ignored. The teenager asking about eating disorder resources? Ignored. But the jewelry brand offering free product? Six-minute response time."

"I can't respond to everyone! Do you know how many DMs—"

"2,847 per day. You responded to three percent. All brands."

"I was running a business!"

"Correct." The Clerk looked up. "You were running a business. Not helping people. There's a difference."

"I inspired people! I made them feel less alone!"

"You made them *think* they knew you. They didn't."

"That's—people loved me!"

"People loved a character you played. Relatable Girl™. Authentic Bestie™. 'My DMs Are Always Open'™. Trademark pending."

"I WAS authentic!"

The Clerk pulled up another screen. "Your 'vulnerable' posts. Therapy mentions: four. All sponsored by BetterHelp. Revenue: $3,200. Actual therapy sessions attended by you: zero."

"That's private!"

"So was your mental health. Until you monetized it."

Jessica felt something cold spreading in her chest. "Everyone does this! Every influencer—"

"Correct. Which is why Hell has a whole wing."

Silence.

The Clerk kept scrolling. "Climate change posts: sixty-seven. Private jet flights that year: sixteen. Carbon footprint: top two percent globally. 'Eco-friendly' water bottle sales: 12,000 units."

"I was doing my best!"

"Your best was three sponsored posts per day and a carbon footprint the size of Nebraska."

"At least I was TRYING to make a difference!"

"Were you trying to make a difference, or trying to look like you were making a difference? Because one requires sacrifice. The other requires a ring light."

Jessica opened her mouth. Nothing came out.

"November 2022," the Clerk said quietly. "A follower's daughter. Suicide. The mother tagged you. Begged you to say something. Her daughter had loved your content. Believed you when you said 'I'm here for you.'"

Jessica went very still.

"You saw it. Your assistant flagged it. You told her to ignore it because you didn't want to 'get involved in something heavy.' Three hours later you posted a make-up tutorial. 'Glowing into the weekend!'"

"I'm not a therapist! I'm not responsible for—"

"You told them you were there for them."

"I meant—"

"You meant it sounded good in a caption."

The words landed like a slap.

The Clerk reached for the stamp. "Jessica White. You sold empathy you didn't feel. You monetized vulnerability you didn't experience. You built a brand on caring about people you didn't care about. Every cause became content. Every tragedy became an engagement opportunity. You didn't raise awareness. You raised your rates."

"But I—"

"You performed caring for people who actually needed it. And when they reached out? You were too busy filming yourself pretending to care about the next thing."

"That's not fair! I couldn't save everyone!"

"You didn't save anyone. You just posted about how important it was that someone should."

The stamp hovered.

"Please—"

"A person who pretends to care while caring only about themselves isn't an influencer. It's a con artist with good lighting."

THUD.

"Hell."

Jessica stared at the stamp. The verdict. The end of her brand.

"For what? For having followers? For making money?"

"For lying." The Clerk's voice was flat. "Every 'I'm here for you' when you weren't. Every 'my DMs are open' when they weren't. Every 'you're not alone' to people you left on read."

"But people learned from me! People discovered—"

"People learned that posting is the same as helping. That awareness without action is somehow virtuous. That performing concern is the same as caring. Congratulations. You taught a generation that looking good is more important than doing good."

The Clerk gestured to the Hell door. "Through there, please. You have people waiting."

"People who actually cared about me?"

"People who thought they did. There's a difference. You made sure they never learned it."

Jessica walked to the door. Slowly. Like she was walking to the camera for a final shot.

But there was no camera.

There never really had been.

Just a ring light and an audience who believed the performance was real.

She pushed the door open.

Another waiting room. Of course.

At least here, nobody would ask her to post about it.

The door closed.

Behind her, the digital chime pinged.

Now serving: 847,304

Jessica looked back at the empty spot where the dog had been earlier.

The only pure thing in the room had already left.

She walked through the door alone.

Episode 13

The Activist

Karen Thornton had been dead for approximately sixteen minutes when she started explaining to everyone why the waiting room was problematic.

"The hierarchical seating arrangement perpetuates ableist assumptions about—"

Nobody was listening.

Judge Blackwell had moved to the far corner. The woman with the rosary had closed her eyes and started praying faster. Even the atheist had relocated to the other side of the room.

Karen didn't notice. Or didn't care.

She'd taken her number—847,304—and immediately started a conversation nobody wanted to have about how the numeric system reinforced capitalist notions of sequential value and if people would just LISTEN she could explain why this entire structure was—

"Could you not," Silas said from his chair.

Karen turned to him. "Actually, as someone who participated in the carceral system by—"

"I murdered someone. I went to prison. I'm in Hell. We're done here."

"But that's exactly what I'm trying to explain! The carceral system itself is—"

"I don't care." Silas closed his eyes, ignoring her.

Karen pivoted to Judge Blackwell. "You. You spent decades perpetuating systemic oppression through—"

"I'm in Hell," Blackwell said flatly. "I'm aware."

"But do you understand WHY? Do you understand the intersectional dynamics of—"

"I understand that you've been dead for sixteen minutes and you've already made the afterlife worse."

Karen's eyes flashed. "Wow. WOW. So we're tone-policing now? We're going to criticize how I—"

"We're criticizing that you won't shut up," the atheist said from across the room. "That's not tone-policing. That's just... policing."

"Actually," Karen said, turning to him, "the use of the word 'policing' in this context trivializes actual police violence and if you'd read the literature you'd understand that—"

Marcus picked up his chair and moved it. Physically. To the other side of the room.

Karen turned to Agnes, who was clutching her rosary and crying quietly.

"The problem with organized religion," Karen began, "is that it's a tool of oppression used to control marginalized communities through—"

"I just wanted to be good," Agnes whispered.

"'Good' is a social construct designed to enforce compliance with patriarchal, heteronormative—"

Agnes started crying harder.

Father Benjamin stood up. "Leave her alone."

"Oh, interesting!" Karen rounded on him. "So now we have a man speaking over me, which is exactly the kind of—"

"I'm not speaking over you. I'm asking you to stop making a crying woman feel worse."

"She's weaponizing her tears! White women have been using tears to silence—"

"She's crying because she's in Hell!" Father Benjamin's voice rose. "Can you just—for one second—can you just let someone exist without lecturing them?!"

Karen opened her mouth.

The digital chime pinged.

NOW SERVING: 847,304.

Everyone in the room looked at each other.

Then at Karen.

Then back at each other.

Nobody said anything.

But the relief was palpable.

Karen walked to the window, already composing her opening statement. The Clerk was about to get an education on why divine judgment was inherently problematic and if he'd just LISTEN she could explain—

The Clerk looked up.

"Karen Thornton."

"Yes, and before we start I need to address the inherent power dynamics in this system because—"

"Activist. Dead at forty-one. Heart attack during an online argument about proper pronoun usage in Spanish."

"It's a gendered language and the colonial implications of—"

"You died mad on the internet."

"I died FIGHTING for—"

The Clerk's fingers moved across the keyboard. "Twelve years of activism. Seventeen causes. Forty-one online campaigns. Six hundred and thirty-two people fired, canceled, or deplatformed."

"I held people accountable!"

"Did you?" The Clerk looked up. "Let's see. May 2016. Your coworker said 'that's crazy' about a deadline. You reported him to HR for ableist language. He got fired. He had three kids."

"Language matters! We can't just—"

"He said 'that's crazy' about a deadline. You got him fired."

"He needed to learn that—"

"August 2017. College student in your activist group said 'you guys' in a meeting. You spent forty minutes explaining why it was exclusionary. She apologized. You said the apology wasn't sufficient and demanded—"

"Apologies need to demonstrate actual understanding of—"

The Clerk looked up.

Karen's mouth sealed shut. Lips fusing together mid-word like someone had hit mute on reality.

Her eyes went wide. She clawed at her face. Tried to scream. Nothing.

"As I was saying," the Clerk continued, looking back at his screen. "You started a campaign to remove her from the organization. She quit activism entirely. Never participated in social justice work again. Because of you."

Karen's mouth opened again. She gasped.

"I suggest you think carefully about what you say next."

"You can't just SILENCE people! That's literally—"

Her mouth sealed again.

"I just did. Twice." The Clerk's voice was flat. "Want to go for three?"

Karen's mouth opened. She stayed silent. Breathing hard.

"Good choice." The Clerk scrolled. "October 2018. Friend shared a BBC article about climate change. You publicly called her out. Tagged her employer. Got her fired."

Karen opened her mouth—

"The article was factually accurate and well-sourced. But the institution had a problematic history. So you destroyed your friend's career over a footnote. Friendship ended. Job gone. All because she shared an article about melting ice caps."

"She was platforming—"

"She shared an article about ice. You ruined her life."

"People need to be held—"

"March 2020. Pandemic. Mutual aid network forming in your community. You joined. Lasted three weeks."

"They weren't centering the right voices! They weren't—"

"They were delivering groceries to elderly people. You spent the entire time explaining why their language was problematic. They asked you to leave."

"Because they couldn't handle being—"

"Because you spent more time policing everyone's words than helping anyone." The Clerk pulled up another document. "July 2021. Sixteen-year-old in your online group used the wrong term. Apologized immediately. You said the apology wasn't enough. Posted their information across platforms. Called for them to be deplatformed."

Karen's face went pale.

"They attempted suicide two weeks later."

Silence.

"They lived. No thanks to you. But you'd already moved on to the next person who needed educating."

"I didn't—I couldn't have—"

"You didn't ask. You didn't care. You saw an opportunity to prove your righteousness and you took it. A sixteen-year-old's mental health was less important than your public stance on terminology."

"I was trying to educate!"

"You were trying to execute." The Clerk looked up. "Education leaves room for growth. You left room for nothing. Perfect compliance or total destruction. Those were the only options."

"I fought for marginalized people!"

"September 2022. A Black woman disagreed with you about racial justice. You—a white woman—spent four hours explaining to her why she was wrong about her own experience. When she pushed back, you called her divisive. Got her removed from the group."

"She was creating horizontal conflict when we need-ed—"

"She disagreed with you. You couldn't handle it. So you weaponized your position as 'ally' to silence her."

"That's not—"

"You spent twelve years calling people out for not be-ing pure enough. You ruined careers. Destroyed friend-ships. Drove a teenager to attempt suicide. And you called it justice."

The Clerk reached for the stamp.

"But I was RIGHT! I was fighting for—"

"For permission to judge everyone. Congratulations. You got it."

The stamp hovered.

"Karen Thornton. You didn't fight oppression. You became it. You didn't build anything. You just burned people down and called it progress. You weaponized every cause you claimed to care about. Used justice as an excuse to be cruel. And convinced yourself that right-eousness was the same as being right."

"Please—I was trying to—"

"You were trying to feel superior. Every call-out was proof of your purity. Every cancellation was proof of your righteousness. You didn't want a better world. You wanted a world where everyone was as miserable as you were."

"NO! I wanted—"

"You wanted to judge. And now you have."

The stamp came down.

THUD.

"Hell."

Karen's mouth opened to argue—

And sealed shut.

Not temporarily this time.

Permanently.

Her lips fused together. Smooth. Seamless. Gone. Like they'd never existed.

Her eyes went wide. Pure, animal panic.

She clawed at her face. Tried to scream. Nothing. Not even muffled sound. Just... silence.

The Clerk didn't look up.

"That's part of your punishment."

Karen stood frozen. Eyes streaming. Hands frantically touching the smooth space where her mouth had been.

"Twelve years of talking over everyone. Silencing people with your voice." The Clerk gestured back toward the waiting room. "Eternity of silence. Seems fair."

He stamped another form.

"Return to the main waiting area. Your door will open when processing is complete."

Karen's eyes went wider. She tried to speak. Nothing.

"I said return to the waiting area."

Karen backed away from the window. Slowly. Hands still on her face. Eyes screaming. Silent.

She walked back to the chairs.
Everyone watched her.
Nobody spoke.
Nobody moved.
They just... stared.
At the smooth space where her mouth had been.
At her panicked eyes.
At her shaking hands.
Karen sat down. As far from everyone else as possible.
Curled into herself. Silent. Forever.

THE END

AUTHOR'S NOTE

You just read thirteen episodes about divine judgment.

Odds are, you saw yourself in at least one of them. Probably more.

That's **UFiction—U**ncomfortable **F**iction. You Fiction. Fiction about You.

It doesn't let you be the observer. It makes you complicit.

The Judge who judged. The Saint who condemned. The Bystander who watched. The Influencer who performed caring. The Activist who weaponized righteousness.

They're all us. On different days. In different situations. When we think no one's counting.

But someone's always counting.

If these episodes made you uncomfortable, good. That means you're paying attention.

The stories continue in 2026.

Join the waiting room at www.elliselms.com

See you there.
— **Ellis Elms**